DIPPING INTO BLOOD
An Anthology of Horror Stories

Edited by Dorothy Davies

DIPPING INTO BLOOD
An Anthology of Horror Stories

GRAVESTONE PRESS

TABLE OF CONTENTS

DEDICATION

This collection is dedicated to Edgar Allen Poe
In his memory we include
The Raven.

Once upon a midnight dreary, while I pondered,
weak and weary,
Over many a quaint and curious volume of
forgotten lore—
While I nodded, nearly napping, suddenly there
came a tapping,
As of some-one gently rapping, rapping at my
chamber door—
"'Tis some visitor," I muttered, "tapping at my
chamber door—
Only this and nothing more."

Ah, distinctly I remember it was in the bleak
December;
And each separate dying ember wrought its ghost
upon the floor.
Eagerly I wished the morrow;—vainly I had sought
to borrow
From my books surcease of sorrow—sorrow for the
lost Lenore—
For the rare and radiant maiden whom the angels
name Lenore—
Nameless *here* for evermore.

And the silken, sad, uncertain rustling of each
purple curtain
Thrilled me—filled me with fantastic terrors never
felt before;
So that now, to still the beating of my heart, I stood
repeating
"'Tis some visitor entreating entrance at my
chamber door—
Some late visitor entreating entrance at my chamber
door;—
This it is and nothing more."

Presently my soul grew stronger; hesitating then no
longer,
"Sir," said I, "or Madam, truly your forgiveness I
implore;
But the fact is I was napping, and so gently you
came rapping,
And so faintly you came tapping, tapping at my
chamber door,

That I scarce was sure I heard you"—here I opened
wide the door;—
Darkness there and nothing more.

Deep into that darkness peering, long I stood there
wondering, fearing,
Doubting, dreaming dreams no mortal ever dared to
dream before;
But the silence was unbroken, and the stillness gave
no token,
And the only word there spoken was the whispered
word, "Lenore?"

This I whispered, and an echo murmured back the
word, "Lenore!"—
Merely this and nothing more.

Back into the chamber turning, all my soul within
me burning,
Soon again I heard a tapping somewhat louder than
before.
"Surely," said I, "surely that is something at my
window lattice;
Let me see, then, what thereat is, and this mystery
explore—
Let my heart be still a moment and this mystery
explore;—
'Tis the wind and nothing more!"

Open here I flung the shutter, when, with many a
flirt and flutter,
In there stepped a stately Raven of the saintly days
of yore;
Not the least obeisance made he; not a minute
stopped or stayed he;
But, with mien of lord or lady, perched above my
chamber door—
Perched upon a bust of Pallas just above my
chamber door—
Perched, and sat, and nothing more.

Then this ebony bird beguiling my sad fancy into
smiling,
By the grave and stern decorum of the countenance
it wore,

"Though thy crest be shorn and shaven, thou," I
said, "art sure no craven,
Ghastly grim and ancient Raven wandering from the
Nightly shore—
Tell me what thy lordly name is on the Night's
Plutonian shore!"
Quoth the Raven "Nevermore."

Much I marvelled this ungainly fowl to hear
discourse so plainly,
Though its answer little meaning—little relevancy
bore;
For we cannot help agreeing that no living human
being
Ever yet was blest with seeing bird above his
chamber door—
Bird or beast upon the sculptured bust above his
chamber door,
With such name as "Nevermore."

But the Raven, sitting lonely on the placid bust,
spoke only
That one word, as if his soul in that one word he did
outpour.
Nothing further then he uttered—not a feather then
he fluttered—
Till I scarcely more than muttered "Other friends
have flown before—
On the morrow *he* will leave me, as my hopes have
flown before."
Then the bird said "Nevermore."

Startled at the stillness broken by reply so aptly
spoken,
"Doubtless," said I, "what it utters is its only stock
and store
Caught from some unhappy master whom
unmerciful Disaster
Followed fast and followed faster till his songs one
burden bore—
Till the dirges of his Hope that melancholy burden
bore
Of 'Never—nevermore.'"

But the Raven still beguiling my sad fancy into
smiling,
Straight I wheeled a cushioned seat in front of bird,
and bust and door;
Then, upon the velvet sinking, I betook myself to
linking
Fancy unto fancy, thinking what this ominous bird
of yore—
What this grim, ungainly, ghastly, gaunt and
ominous bird of yore
Meant in croaking "Nevermore."

This I sat engaged in guessing, but no syllable
expressing
To the fowl whose fiery eyes now burned into my
bosom's core;
This and more I sat divining, with my head at ease
reclining
On the cushion's velvet lining that the lamp-light
gloated o'er,

But whose velvet violet lining with the lamp-light
gloating o'er,
She shall press, ah, nevermore!

Then, methought, the air grew denser, perfumed
from an unseen censer
Swung by Seraphim whose foot-falls tinkled on the
tufted floor.
"Wretch," I cried, "thy God hath lent thee—by these
angels he hath sent thee
Respite—respite and nepenthe, from thy memories
of Lenore;
Quaff, oh quaff this kind nepenthe and forget this
lost Lenore!"
Quoth the Raven "Nevermore."

"Prophet!" said I, "thing of evil!—prophet still, if
bird or devil!—
Whether Tempter sent, or whether tempest tossed
thee here ashore,
Desolate yet all undaunted, on this desert land
enchanted—
On this home by Horror haunted—tell me truly, I
implore—
Is there—is there balm in Gilead?—tell me—tell
me, I implore!"
Quoth the Raven "Nevermore."

"Prophet!" said I, "thing of evil—prophet still, if
bird or devil!
By that Heaven that bends above us—by that God
we both adore—

Tell this soul with sorrow laden if, within the distant
Aidenn,
It shall clasp a sainted maiden whom the angels
name Lenore—
Clasp a rare and radiant maiden whom the angels
name Lenore."
Quoth the Raven "Nevermore."

"Be that word our sign in parting, bird or fiend!" I
shrieked, upstarting—
"Get thee back into the tempest and the Night's
Plutonian shore!
Leave no black plume as a token of that lie thy soul
hath spoken!
Leave my loneliness unbroken!—quit the bust
above my door!
Take thy beak from out my heart, and take thy form
from off my door!"
Quoth the Raven "Nevermore."

And the Raven, never flitting, still is sitting, *still* is
sitting
On the pallid bust of Pallas just above my chamber
door;
And his eyes have all the seeming of a demon's that
is dreaming,
And the lamp-light o'er him streaming throws his
shadow on the floor;
And my soul from out that shadow that lies floating
on the floor
Shall be lifted—nevermore!

Imminent Signs

Gary Budgen

Ed, my Ed, speaks to me. Ever since the incident on the platform he's spoken to me, telling me things I otherwise wouldn't know.

On the bus.

"Look at him over there, with the odd socks. You know who goes out with odd socks?"

"No." I murmur because I can't be seen talking to myself.

"It's a signal. It's to let others in the know understand he's part of a secret group involved in the killing of something."

"The killing of what?"

"Well, the higher the life-form the greater the prestige. They start with inconsequential things when they're children, ants, beetles. They might dismember a butterfly by pulling off its wings. Then they move onto their pets, cats, dogs, rabbits. Anything they can get their hands on. They're building up to the murder of a human being, which will assure their place in the ranks of the Order."

"The Order?"

"Be quiet. He's looking at you. He knows we're onto him."

I want to ask what I should do. I surely have to act.

When the man with odd socks gets off I follow. We're somewhere in central London.

"It's no good, they're everywhere," says Ed.

"What do you mean they're everywhere? I can't see anyone else with odd socks."

"There are other signs."

"What?"

A pair of young Japanese woman are staring at me. There is a sharp pain in my temples. Ed is angry. Now, I know, he will not speak, but instead retreat somewhere inside, leaving only this pain which might last for days. The sky is too close and all around there are people staring. I can feel the panic accelerating along with the pain in my head. By the time I get home all I can do is lie down in darkness.

***

I research the internet for information on the headaches. I think about contacting the doctors and pick up my phone several times to dial. But then Ed comes back.

"What are you doing?"

"I just… I think I ought to…"

"You haven't got time to waste. Do you want innocent people out there to be murdered?"

"No…"

"Well, get a move on."

There are other signs. People wearing only one glove. Carrying an umbrella they never use. Scratching through their clothing. Lingering too long in front of advertising hoardings. Thus the

15

members of the Order indicate their presence to each other.

"The best thing you can do," says Ed, "is to find someone who is at the point of acting. And for that the signs are particular. They're called imminent. They need to be differentiated from the preliminary signs I've told you about."

"But…"

"What?"

"Can't we just go to the police?"

"Don't be stupid. The police are in on it."

"But… I'm scared."

"What do you have to be scared about? Haven't I always looked after you?"

This is true. Ever since the station platform, Ed has been there. It was night when I got out of the train. I walked down the platform and became aware of something behind me. Then there was a sudden blow and dizziness. As I fell I heard quick, urgent, instructions. Kick his head. Get his phone. Get his wallet. His head. Ed. My Ed. Beginning as a pain along the side of my temple, forming words, the voice that would look after me.

"How do I stop the murders?"

"If you can stop one of them it'll send a message to the rest. It'll make them understand someone is standing up to them. They'll go into hiding."

"Tell me about the imminent signs."

An imminent sign is more subtle but it displays a sense of purpose. A person using an imminent sign might be walking just a little too fast, not looking left or right but only ahead as though

16

nothing else around them matters. They might, occasionally, glance at a wrist watch, but this is all bluff. What matters is not the time itself but the moments counting down to the murder.

I soon find one of them. A man in a dark suit with shiny black shoes. With neat hair. I have the sharpened carving knife in my pocket, because, as Ed says, there is nothing wrong with taking a life in order to save the life of an innocent.

I follow the man down the High Street. Then into the little park near the train station.

"You're doing really well," says Ed.

The man stops, he looks at his wrist watch. It's all just as Ed has said. Then he goes towards the public toilets.

"This is it. You have to act now."

I follow the man towards the toilets. I am going to do it. I am going to save a life. But then just before I go in Ed retreats. There are no words, only pain. All across my skull there is only searing pain and a threat of darkness. Worse than anything I have felt before.

"Ed!"

The man, the man who has just murdered an innocent person in the toilet, is standing before me.

"You're bleeding" he says, "I think I'd better call an ambulance."

I feel it. Creeping across my face, flowing from my nose and from my eyes. Warmly caressing yet tasting of the iron of resolve. In my moment of need Ed has come out into the world.

17

The Most Horrible Thing

Terrance V. Mc Arthur

It was a dream.
I think it was a dream.
I hope it was a dream.

I stood in an amusement park, in front of a ride. The sign read "The Most Horrible Thing." A string of cars waited for passengers. It jolted into action, empty, rumbling toward a dark tunnel. Suddenly I wanted to know what waited at the end of that tunnel. I vaulted over the railing, clambered into the last car, then watched as the safety bar closed over my lap. The chain of cars rolled into the darkness and I called out, "Go ahead! Show me The Most Horrible Thing!"

No voice replied. Letters shone above me, glaring out of the black void:

"IT BEGINS"

I saw tiny creatures, an indistinct blackness with red, glowing eyes. At first, they only attacked small animals of the woodland, shredding squirrels and little birds into messes of blood and fur or feathers. When the petite invaders ranged out into the meadows, they encountered sheep. Displays of the carnage included missing heads, piles of bones and the silhouette of a frantic ram struggling to escape while the muscles of its legs were gnawed off below it by blobs of darkness, red eyes bobbing, pursuing and gutting their quarry.

Before long, the dark creatures took on a herd of cattle. Entrails spattered the rocks and trees. Knots of creatures separated a cow from her calf. One carcass lay on its back, legs jiggling in the air, its distended belly fluttering from the movements of the little monsters chewing from the inside, while the hide lit from within by flashes of red light. In the distance could be seen the farms and towns of a new and intriguing kind of prey: Man.

In the darkness, another message glowed into life:

"THEY ATTACK"

"Come on," I shouted. "Enough, already! Show me The Most Horrible Thing!"

My demand ignored, the letters faded into black. A new set of scenes began.

Dead bodies lay thrown about like discarded candy wrappers. Certain themes emerged. I saw lots of guts and intestines, with decapitations making a strong showing. One headless body hung upside-down, the blood dripping into a lumpy, clotted pool of reddish-brown goo, where creatures of blackness lapped up the gore, their red eyes glowing with desire and satisfaction.

The scene darkened. I thought the section had come to an end, but there was one more tableau to see. Terrified children peered out from a kitchen cupboard at the mutilated body of their mother. She shuddered with her last breaths, but there was a look of triumph on her face. The source of her satisfaction: she clutched one of the creatures in her fist and the dark attacker's red glow dimmed, becoming dull and glazed.

"THE PEOPLE FIGHT BACK"

I sat in silence. The car rumbled toward new displays and situations. They still showed death and destruction, savaged humans and I still faced the headless and disemboweled, but things had changed. More dark creatures were among the dead, singly at first, then in pairs and trios, until a whole herd of them lay squashed like blackish melons beneath a rock, the luster fading from their eyes.

I wondered, "What now?" In answer, letters in the darkness:

"THE WAR IS OVER"

A town square, almost the model of traditional, small-town American innocence and pride, but it seemed a mockery of the Mayberry/Norman Rockwell ideal. Dry and gray-leafed trees, paint peeling from the old-time bandstand and the dirty banner overhead, inexpertly painted and misspelled: "VIKTERY." The people...

Did I really want to see The Most Horrible Thing after all?

Tired, haggard, bony frames holding up ragged clothes, as if their souls shrunk with their bodies and the children...

"LOOK AT THE CHILDREN"

...the children... children... stunted... bloated bellies... twisted...

I didn't know what I wanted, any more, but I did not want to see The Most Horrible Thing and I definitely did not want to look at the children. I wanted to look at anything else and I frantically searched for something to see. I settled on a young mother, pale and gaunt yet serenely hopeful, fiercely holding and protecting her sleeping baby. The baby... the baby... Delicate and pink, new and fragile, wrapped in a torn, faded blanket. He stirred in her arms, opened his eyes... his eyes... and I woke screaming and crying, but I still could see the baby's red, glowing eyes.

Next!

Dorothy Davies

It was almost impossible to get a toe inside the room, let alone actually go in, but if I wasn't inside, how would I hear my name called? I had no plans to spend eternity on the outside; I needed to know where I was going and who I was going with. Admittedly the second part was relatively incidental, eternity was eternity even if I liked the person /people.

I pushed a little harder.

"Give over!" someone muttered. "There's no room!"

But at that moment I heard "NEXT!" shouted from the other end and everyone moved up a fraction, just enough to let me in.

Just my luck to die when there was – seemingly – a plane crash, a capsized cruise liner and a train wreck all at the same time. That was my first impression, considering how many spirits were crammed into the large area. Some were holding steering wheels, some had half a face where they'd been burned; some had holes where knives or bullets had entered. It took me about five minutes, if I remember what five minutes felt like, to realize there were no major disasters, this was the usual amount of people trying to find their destination after death. The second thing I realized was that everyone there, including me, had died violently. There were no cancer or heart victims or those who had died of sheer old age among this crowd. Everyone carried signs of violence of some kind or another.

Interesting.

Well, for someone who likes people watching, it is.

Ha! Amend that. Spirit watching.

"Move up!" someone grunted but no one shifted an inch. We couldn't. There was no room.

"Move up!" The voice got louder. It produced a chorus of "Push off! No room! What do you think we're doing, standing around like this for our health?" and other such comments. Some were unrepeatable. People don't change when they cross over, that was blatantly obvious. I heard words I'd never heard before, some actually made me blush. I thought I couldn't be shocked by anything anymore.

Not after Arthur Menton killed me.

Look at that, would you? I said his name without spitting blood or curses or both. I seem to have mellowed a little in the few minutes since dying and arriving here. Well, at least one person has mellowed: judging by the sound of the profanities and abuse going on around me, few of the others have.

Nothing changes.

Same old - same old.

I'd hoped for better… but then, I should have known better, shouldn't I? Been told enough times from the platform in all those spiritualist meetings, our loved ones don't change when they get to the other side. Nor do our hated ones, it seems.

I'm saying that because I've just spotted Arthur Menton in the crowd. Ha! So I did do him in as he did me in, after all! Thank everything that needs to be thanked for that small mercy. I can face eternity better knowing he isn't walking the earth plane whilst I'm crammed in this room/way centre/gathering place/whatever it is waiting for someone to tell me where I'm going. And he's pushing and shoving and swearing just as he did before I carved him up from navel to throat. Never thought I had it in me.

"Next!"

We all moved along a fraction and Menton came closer to me, eyes glittering with hate, just as they did half an hour earlier. It's no more than that since we arrived here.

"You..." He begans his curses again, but someone thumped him in the ribs, hard.

"Shut it, big mouth! We're all dead! Chew on that and wait your turn!"

Surprisingly, he does. The mouth slams shut like a vault – my wish is to turn the huge handle slowly and carefully, only with him inside it.

We're all dead. Chew on that and wait your turn.

I'm as guilty as him in thinking we're still alive.

Just when I thought we would all be stood there for days, if not weeks, as we were selected for this or that destination, something happened that took me – and a lot of others – completely by surprise. A bunch of hooded skeletons with grinning skulls fought their way in. Actually, despite the crush, it wasn't difficult for them as you took one look and, space or no space, you moved back.

They stormed through, bony fingers reaching out touching this one, that one, a tap on the head, on the shoulder, on the nose and that person followed them obediently, as if drugged. Arthur Menton was one of them. No fight left, just puppy-dog devotion following the black robe through the crowd which eased back to let them pass. By then there was a lot of room, they took a whole swathe with them.

"Heading for hell," someone commented behind me. "No need for selection for them, their deeds signposted their destination before they got here."

That left me wondering where I was going. I had been guilty of killing as much as he had, only –

Mine was self-defence. His was out and out murder for the sake of it. All I had done was criticise his car.

Wouldn't you? I mean, a bright yellow thing with spoilers and big fat tyres and a horn that played a ridiculous tune…

It was his bad luck I had a Stanley knife in my pocket.

I was a good deal closer to the door now, awaiting that 'Next!' call.

And getting scared.

Stupid, isn't it? I mean, there I am, stone dead, standing in a waiting room of stone dead, worrying about where I'm going…

Ha! The alternative has arrived. The alternative to the skeletons, that is. Golden haired white robed beings with bland benign faces; the ones I hate as they reveal absolutely nothing. That means you have to work twice as hard to find out what they're thinking. Whatever... they walked through, touching this one, that one, muttering names under their breath, until they had a whole crowd which followed them out of the room.

"Heading for heaven," said the same voice which said Menton and others were heading for hell.

I turned round. Yes, there was that much room now I could do that. I looked into a face that was vaguely familiar but then again could have been the face on a hundred people during my life. Ordinary, comfortable, aged, you know the type.

"Hallo, mate!"

A chubby hand thrust at me. I took it without thinking. "Hallo back to you," I said, desperately trying to remember who he was.

"You don't really remember me, do you?"

"Well ... you're very familiar, I have to say that."

"I should be. I delivered your mail for almost a quarter of a century. More times than not you didn't see me. I was up too early for you, in the days when the postman came early and didn't knock at all."

"I thought this was a waiting room for those who died violently."

"I did. Irate householder with an equally irate guard dog. Got me, so it did."

"Sorry about that."

26

"I'm not. Sick to death – excuse the pun – of the job and the customers and the gates which jammed and letter boxes which trapped my fingers. This way I got out of the job and the Missus got the compensation."

"But – you've left her on her own!"

"It won't be long before she's over here too. Bad heart, bad kidneys, bad back, you name it, she's got it bad."

"Look, I know this sounds stupid, but you don't know where you're going, so how will she find you?"

"Who said anything about wanting her to find me?"

"Oh. Right."

"Next!"

We moved up a bit more.

The room was emptying out fast. I hadn't seen where some of the dead had gone, those not collected by the skeletons or the angels, definitely not gone through that menacing door, where the man shouts "Next!" like some sergeant-major or something. They were just – not there anymore. I wondered if they found their destination. Was there a map on the wall, like one of the underground system, they chose somewhere and just – went?

I turned to ask someone but I was suddenly, surprisingly, alone.

The room was vast, cathedral-like in its space and echo-ness. The floor, I realized, was marked out in concentric circles and spirals which would drive you insane if you decided to walk them. I didn't try. I stood in the corner by the door, which held even more menace than it had before, and tried to look innocuous and innocent and timid and everything that would avoid one of those skeletal people coming to tap me on the shoulder or somewhere.

The door opened and a smiling man sporting a pocket stuffed full of pens looked at me.

"Come in."

"Thank… thank you."

"Sit. Don't be scared. Nothing's going to happen you don't agree to."

He sat behind a huge, and I mean huge, desk. You could have landed a 747 on it and had room to spare, I swear that's true. Well, all right, not quite but you get the idea. There was not a scrap of paper on it, no telephone, intercom, nothing. Just a vast expanse of fine grained wood.

I looked at the man. He was still smiling, his shock of pure white hair was every which way, his eyes were twinkling, well, if I said he could have been an understudy for St Nicholas, you get the idea. All he needed was the beard.

"Process of elimination," he said, chuckling.

Can you do that? Talk and chuckle at the same time? He did.

"I'm not entirely…"

"No, of course not. Let me explain. First everyone arrives. Then the hell-bound go to hell. Then the heaven-bound go to heaven. Then the others sort of drift away, knowing where they're going. 99% of them are going back to what we could call real life, to start over again. Reincarnation. It's real, believe me."

"What about the ones you called in by shouting 'Next!' Where did they go?"

"Ah, yes. The Next. I bet you thought every last one of you had to come in, be interviewed and sent on your way, right?"

"Right."

"Wrong. What happened each time I shouted was one individual came forward, someone a bit special, someone who had a pivotal role to play somewhere. They were sent for special training before going back to start a new life. They're your leaders, your movers and shakers, the ones who really get things done."

"I see."

And I did.

"So…"

"Where does that leave you? Last man standing? Simple. I want to give up this job. I'm tired of it, been here about a thousand years now, I want to go do something else. I understand God needs a secretary…" He patted the pens. "I'm good at taking notes, keeping appointment diaries, being an organizer. I've been asked to move on. But I couldn't move on until I found someone to take over. Would you like the job?"

"What do I have to do?"

"Open the door and shout Next! and see who comes forward. Tick their name off the list – it's right here in the drawer – and see them on their way. Be friendly, calming, comforting… I suggest you grow a beard or something, make yourself less daunting. You're a fine looking man but you look a bit fierce with that jutting jaw. You can have the job for as long as you want. All you have to do when you want to move on is ask what vacancies there are in heaven and find someone to take your place."

"Is it really that easy?"

"Try it."

"What – now?"

"Sure. Go open the door, see who's out there. Shout 'Next!' and see who comes in."

"Where will you be?"

"On my way to God's apartment."

I decided to take the job. I mean, why not? I'd been Last Man Standing: someone chose me for it; so I might as well do it. I had nothing to lose, did I?

I went to the door and opened it.

The place was packed...

Hunting Demons

Justin Boote

I told him he should never have played with the Ouija board then all this wouldn't have happened. Just because my brother's fifteen, two years older than me, doesn't make him any cleverer and this proves it.

He's in Mum's arms now like a little baby. Screaming that something reached out and grabbed his foot while he was asleep. Tried to pull him out of bed. I can hear Mum trying to calm him down and tell him he had a nightmare, but he won't listen. He knows the truth, that's why. It's happened too often for it to be a dream.

It was his idea, anyway. He found the Ouija board and said we should give it a go. For a laugh. Well, when the light bulb smashed and showered us in glass and the dark shadow appeared over in the corner, he stopped laughing. He'd been trying to call up some demon he'd heard mentioned in a movie. Can't be real, he said, because monsters in movies are make-believe. Demons don't even exist in the real world.

Yet there it was.

But even then we didn't really believe it. At least I didn't. It was our imaginations, I said. Light bulbs explode all the time; if you look hard enough, you'll find scary shadows everywhere. I know I used to. Then, a few days later he started waking up in the middle of the night. Something was watching him from the closet. He could see a pale face, two eyes bright and terrible, huge and wide, staring back at him. It opened the closet door with fingers like talons and whispered his name. Only then did he run screaming to Mum. Me, I laughed. Wimp.

Mum started getting worried when he said it was happening every night. That it was getting closer: he could smell its foul breath and its outstretched hand scratched at his leg. She took him to the doctor who said there was nothing wrong with him; that he should stop watching horror movies. He prescribed some mild pills to help him sleep. They didn't work.

A few nights later, it almost got him. He was lying in bed, snoring, when the covers were thrown to the floor. A hand, grimy and rough, grabbed him round the throat and started choking him. He opened his eyes, tried to scream, but could only cough and splutter as the thing laughed at him and sang his name over and over. My brother could feel his face burn, his brain throb with the intensity. He pissed the bed, he said, but I didn't laugh. It did sound quite frightening. And then, when he thought he was gonna die or become possessed by the demon, Mum walked in.

She said she saw nothing, but she looked terrified and there was a mark around his throat. Like someone had tried to strangle him with thick rope. I was shocked. After that, things died down for a while. Maybe it had been shocked itself after Mum almost caught it. Maybe it wouldn't be so much fun anymore if anyone other than my brother knew about it. That's what I think, anyway.

That was until tonight. And man, did it come back with a vengeance! How my brother screamed when he saw it again! He thought it had gone for good. I heard him praying for that after the last time. When it touched his foot and whispered in his ear that it was back, that it was going to make him suffer and scream, that the doors of hell were wide open waiting for him. That'd he'd be there for all eternity. Fifteen years old and he still pissed himself like a baby.

What I think is this, though; sometimes people deserve such things to happen to them.   To   be taught a lesson.

It had been him with the stupid idea of using the Ouija board, not me. To attract that presence and all that came after it. And who was the one made to pay for it? Exactly.

So really, all things considered, he brought it on himself, didn't he?

And for not coming to my funeral.

Messy Little Lives

Dan Allen

Because hell, hell is for children
And you know that their little lives can become
such a mess
Pat Benatar

Why do my parents try to protect me from the truth? I understand more than they're willing to accept and my little brain is good at filling in missing details. Details scarier than anything they could share. If they only knew how I suffer.

My mother shields my eyes during the dirty part of a movie. When we drive past an accident on the highway, her hand covers my face. She doesn't get it. My imagination is far more vivid than a glimpse of naked skin or a mangled body lying on the ground.

Now this same imagination is running wild again. I'm still waiting for my ride home from kindergarten. The other kids are long gone and soon a teacher will come out and start bugging me. My mother's late and I don't like being alone. It's boring.

My dad drives a 1965 Baby blue Ford Galaxy 500. I recognize our car before it even stops at the curb. It has seat belts, but I never wear them. I liked

34

riding in the front, standing on the seat and holding on to the dash. Dad waits behind the wheel while I let myself in.

"Hi, Daddy. Where's Mom?"

He doesn't answer, doesn't even look at me. He's wearing his pyjamas, but that's not what worries me.

"Dad?"

"She's at home," he mumbles.

His face is scruffy and covered in whiskers. Didn't he go to work today? Maybe not. Maybe that's what *fired* means. They don't want me to know, but I heard them arguing in the night.

The steering wheel is wet and looks sticky. Dad's hands are covered with a dark glistening fluid like he's been changing the oil. Something drips from his palm and stains his flannel sleeve. Bright red? I'm not going to think about it.

We pull up at our house on Westley Avenue and find the police are waiting for us. Red lights flash everywhere. It's all very exciting, at least until Ambulance guys carry out someone on a stretcher. A sheet covers the body: I can't see who it is.

Cops close in on our car and I realize they aren't here to help. They point their guns at Daddy before he can get the baby blue Ford shut off. They don't even give him a chance to open the door before they drag him out and pin him to the ground. A pair of thick hands grab my shoulders and lift me in the air. I kick and scream and fight bravely. I watch them put Dad in the backseat of a black and white. As they pull onto the road, Dad makes eye contact. He doesn't smile. I don't cry. I probably should.

A horn blasts and shakes me out of my daydream. Mother has finally arrived. I wonder why she's late. I could ask, but I doubt I'll get the truth. My parents lie to me. They say they don't want me to worry. If they only knew.

Promises, Promises

Paul Edwards

Robin's memories had a habit of tearing him apart.

He remembered something that evening, of being back home, sitting at the table all set for supper. Robin and his sister Lucille had ripped into the pizza and garlic bread, loading their plates before Mum and Dad could get a look in.

"Steady on!" Dad'd cried. "Save some for the rest of us."

Robin had given Lucille a wink, then they'd both snatched out, grabbing more, chuckling mischievously at the shock on their parents' faces.

Robin could recall the night's conversation – Lucille's frustrations with her best friend Emma, who liked a boy in their class but was too scared to ask him out; Mum and Dad reminiscing over their university days and how excited they were about Robin going in two years' time; Robin debating whether or not to do an English degree, or follow his heart and study Drama.

"We'll be behind you 100%," Mum'd said. "In whatever you choose to do."

Robin stood up, gasping, panting, feeling like he was on the verge of panic. He needed something to stop himself from thinking they weren't his family anymore, just people he'd dropped from his life. He stumbled into the bathroom, lifted the toilet seat. He tried to be sick, but could only spit and dry heave. Finally, he curled up on the tiled floor and surprised himself by crying, tears cascading down his cheeks in a flood.

When he next opened his eyes, it was some time in the early evening. The sun was setting outside the window. He sat up, groaning, palming drool from off his lips. A knock snatched his attention to the front door. He found his slightly groggy feet.

Standing in the porch was a woman in her thirties, her hair cut in a bob and a lanyard with a card attached looped around her neck. Beside her stood a police officer, also female, slightly older with mousey hair tied in a bun.

The woman with the lanyard held up her card. "Robin Dempsey?"

Robin blinked at the photograph displayed before him.

"I'm Dawn Macready, social worker. This," she nodded at her companion, "is PC Sue Lacock." She turned to Robin again. "May we come in?"

He widened the door and the two women slipped inside. They took a seat on the beat-up sofa. He sat opposite on a stool, gripping his knees to stop himself from shaking.

Dawn glanced about the room. "How long have you been here, Robin?"

"A month."

"It's nice," she said. "You managing the rent okay?"

"Just about."

Sue took her hat off and [ut it in her lap, resting her hands on top. "The purpose of our visit is to check in on you. A routine welfare call, that's all."

Robin remained silent.

"Dawn's going to be working with you from now on. She's going to help you get back on track. Help you turn your life around. How does that sound?"

Robin stared at the WPC, saying nothing.

"You can start by giving us names," Sue continued. "Don't worry, we'll make sure you're safe. That nothing comes back at you."

He noticed a small sweat moustache glistening above her top lip. "Don't what you're talking about," he said.

Sue's voice changed, its tone taking on an air of gravity and menace. "Do you know what the custodial sentence is for the supply of Class A drugs?" She didn't wait for an answer. "Thirty years. Do you want that for yourself, Robin?"

She left a pause which Robin was unwilling to fill.

"You're just a kid," she said, shaking her head from side to side. "They've taken advantage of you."

Robin wasn't going to fall for this – he'd made promises and the consequences of breaking those promises kept him up at night.

"Robin," Dawn leaned forward. "We can help. Just… let us in, okay? Let us work with you. We'll leave our contact information here, so you can get in touch at any time. And you need to start attending the rehabilitation programme, okay?"

"Are you still using?" Sue asked him.

He looked up, then flinched away from her gaze. "No."

"Are you in trouble with your suppliers? I mean, after what was seized?"

Robin responded by shaking his head.

Another pause.

"I'll be making regular house calls," Dawn said. "I'll work hard for you. But I need you to meet me halfway, okay? You need to work with me. It doesn't have to be like this. *Promise,* Robin."

***

The call came two days later – a loud, abrupt thump on his door. Robin jumped out of the sofa, shuffling toward the jittery-looking shadow beyond the door's frosted glass.

He opened up. A young man with a thin, pasty-looking face grinned in at him. "Rob?"

Robin nodded. He glanced outside to ensure no one was watching, then ushered the youth in, closing and locking the door behind him.

"We heard we could trust you," the young man said, seating himself right on the edge of the sofa. "Heard you could help us out. Like you helped us out the other day, right?" He stuck out his hand. "Charley's the name."

Robin bent forward, shaking it. It felt unpleasantly clammy and warm.

"Do you..." Charley began.

"Oh." Robin pointed toward the bedroom. "I'll go get your money."

"No rush. No rush, man."

Robin ran into his bedroom, grabbed a belt bag and brought it in with him to the front room. He unzipped it before putting it on the coffee table. Charley stood, counting the notes inside. Most of it was Robin's savings; the last of his own money that he'd stashed away. The police had seized the rest.

"Sweet," Charley said, stuffing the notes into the pockets of his jacket. "Think you'll do us just fine." His smile grew larger. "Play your cards right and you could be one of us. We're one big happy family here."

"Cool." Robin bit at his nails. "Do you have anything for me?"

"Sorry, man." Charley gave an apologetic shrug. "Just waiting on the new batch to arrive. Should be here tomorrow, though."

Tremors of anxiety coursed through Robin. "What time tomorrow?"

"Can't promise a time, mate. I'll get to you when I can." Charley got to his feet, patting the notes inside his pockets. "It's not what you think it is, you know."

"Sorry?"

"The pills. They help us get bigger... Stronger, too. It's our way of recruiting and instilling obedience and fear." He pressed a finger to his lips. "Keep quiet, though. We don't talk to anyone outside the fam about it. We're always watching; always listening. You're either with us, or you ain't. But I wouldn't want to be you if you ain't, bro."

41

Charley's visit had made Robin feel massively paranoid. He was angry about not getting what he was owed, too. He knew the pills had become an addiction; he'd even got used to the fucked up hallucinations that came with them. Usually, these visions revolved around being chased by some sort of *thing,* its many hands reaching out, its many mouths calling for him, *hungering* for him.

Robin dragged a hand through greasy knots of his hair. He had a small amount of money left, which would help get him drunk at the pub in the village. He didn't like the idea of going out, but didn't like the idea of staying in, either. He'd only start thinking about his family again.

He left his lodgings and followed a winding country lane to the Centurion Inn. The sky was grey, barely seeming real at all. The village streets were deserted. Behind the cluster of houses, he could see the church steeple and the landmark known as Congress Hill.

The pub's interior was no less drab. Farming tools and implements dressed the walls. Two ruddy-faced men were huddled in a corner, nursing pints of cider. Another man with a thick knotted beard was propping up the bar, talking to the elderly landlord.

Robin approached, digging into his pockets for change.

The landlord lifted his arms, straightening. "What can I get you, young man?"

"Cider," Robin said. "A double whisky too, please."

42

"You eighteen?"

Robin nodded, and the landlord and customer at the bar exchanged smirks.

The customer turned to him and said, "Haven't seen you around before."

"I'm in The Retreat."

"Ah," the man said, scratching his beard. "Social Services are always putting kids into that place. Not the most appropriate of accommodations, if you ask me."

The landlord came over, setting the drinks down in front of Robin who knocked back the whisky, then took a couple of steady gulps of cider.

The man at the bar watched on, a wry smile stitched to his lips. "Thirsty?"

"Yeah." Robin gestured to the man's glass. "Can I get you one?"

"That's very sporting of you." He turned to the landlord. "Same again, John."

The landlord shuffled off to refill the man's glass, while Robin began hesitant conversation. He didn't really want to be talking; he just wanted to get blindingly drunk here. But he wondered if conversing with others might actually do him some good. Help stop him obsessing over the same thoughts, the same feelings, all the time.

The man introduced himself as Jim, a local farmer. "Thought you were one of *them* when you first came in," he said. "Those fucking druggies up in the old Morgan house on Congress Hill. It's not much of a house, mind you. More like a shell of one. Reckon God threw a hissy fit over what was going on up there and chucked a lightning bolt at

43

it." Jim ran a finger around the rim of his pint glass. "Old Morgan's a funny bird, mind. Won't have anything to do with us in the village. But then, we don't have much to do with him, either. We hear him, though – when the wind's blowing right, ranting and raving like a mad man."

"Congress Hill's got a reputation for being haunted," John said from behind the counter.

"Haunted?" Robin asked.

"There's been stories about that hill, going back centuries. Remember my gramps telling us it was cursed and not to go up there at certain times of year."

"Watch yourself, lad," Jim nodded. "Morgan and his missus are up there taking in all manner of waifs and strays. Which is weird, 'cause his house looks completely uninhabitable. The police won't look into it too deeply, of course. We thought about rounding up the village and going up there ourselves, but folk are scared of what they'll find. So, no one does a thing. But, just lately, things have been getting worse. Hearing 'em more, too…"

A youth in a hoodie suddenly burst through the door, looking sweaty and pale, heading straight for the bar. He ordered himself a gin, then took it over to a table by the fireplace.

It was getting late, darkness gathering and pressing up against the windows.

"Know him?" Jim asked, nodding over Robin's shoulder.

Robin glanced around, disturbed to see the youth was staring right at him.

"He's one of them," Jim sniffed. "You can tell by looking at him." He blinked and gazed at Robin again. "You definitely not one of them? He's taken a keen interest in you, lad. And now that I mention it, you're not looking in the best of health yourself, you know."

Robin was home half an hour later, unable to shake off a strange and dislocating sense of dread. It cut through the booze, sobering him, nullifying the effects of the alcohol. He crashed out on the sofa, wishing his brain to shut up long enough for him to sleep.

Perhaps he could write a letter. Make a call in the phone box in the village. That was all it might take. But would his parents take him back? He knew he'd said some pretty awful things to them. Stolen from them, too.

Maybe he was only thinking like this because he'd been drinking. At least the pills blacked everything out for a while.

He was finally beginning to doze when a knock startled him awake again.

Charley was at the door. "Alright, Rob?"

"Hey." Robin frowned, holding the door open. "Thought you were coming tomorrow."

"I was. But I managed to get hold of your gear a little earlier than expected." He took a polythene packet out of his jacket pocket, handing it to Robin. "Just a couple for now."

"Only a couple?"

"Might have more for you to push soon. They want you to take another trip into the city."

45

Robin nodded, but wasn't sure if he could, or would, help next time.

Charley glanced over both his shoulders, then fixed Robin with a pointed gaze. "Listen, I want you to meet the rest of the gang. Come along to a party we're having tomorrow. It's been a while since we've had anyone new."

"Where?"

"Congress Hill."

Robin felt the hairs on the back of his neck stand on end.

"We're going to meet in the old house up there. Come about nine, okay?" He nodded at the packet in Robin's hand. "I'll make sure you get everything you're owed."

Charley pointed a finger at him as he walked away. "You'll be there, right?"

"Course."

"Good man." Charley's eyes glittered above his vaguely grotesque smile. "Just bring yourself. Can't wait to see you there. It's going to be one hell of a party."

***

The pills took him to where he needed to be – spaced out, wasted, and numb. But at some point in the night, he was aware of being chased by something alien through claustrophobic darkness, its hands reaching, its myriad mouths salivating, hungering for him. When he finally came down, it was mid-morning and he was wrapped in a sweat-sodden sheet. He realised from the mess in the toilet that he'd vomited and his reflection in the mirror was gaunt, pale and wraithlike.

He recalled Charley's visit as he cleaned and the plan to meet the rest of the gang on Congress Hill. He didn't have to go; he could just leave this place and never come back. But he didn't trust himself. Not when he was so dependent on the pills. He was still owed more and he was going to make damned sure he got them all.

Later he was awakened by a persistent knock on his door. He thought it might be Charley, calling round to see if Robin was still coming tonight. But when he opened up, he was shocked and surprised to see Dawn, the social worker. She was on her own this time.

"May I come in?

Robin opened the door wide.

She stepped tentatively inside. "How've you been?"

"Fine."

She sat down on the sofa. "No offence, but you're not looking so great, Robin." When he didn't say anything, she produced a small, strained smile. "I've sorted taxis out for you. They'll come at eight-thirty every Tuesday morning. I'll meet you after your first rehabilitation session, which is this Tuesday coming. We'll talk in an office next to the classroom, okay?"

Robin nodded, "Sure," knowing full well he wouldn't be there.

"Great." Dawn forced her smile to look a little bigger, a little brighter. "We can put a plan together. Identify areas where we can make some positive changes." She adjusted her lanyard, sitting back a little. "I spoke to your parents the other day."

It felt as if thousands of tiny invisible spiders had just run up his spine.

"They felt reassured you're safe," she continued. "That you're getting the help you need."

"Why would you do that?"

"Because I wanted to see if they would consider offering you any help before I talked it through with you."

"Shouldn't you have done that the other way around?"

Dawn didn't reply.

She smiled again, but this time her smile was a lot fainter and forlorn looking. "Your parents asked lots of questions, many of which I couldn't answer. But, despite all that's happened – and I don't know a lot, Robin, *honest* – they say they love you and they'd take you back in a shot."

"I don't want them to take me back."

"Would you consider talking to them? Just over the phone, I mean. I haven't told them where you are. I wouldn't do that without your permission."

Heavy silence descended. Robin couldn't think of anything to say. Finally, Dawn sighed and said, "They're confused and hurt and they never wanted you out of their lives like this. I think…"

Suddenly, he burst into tears; couldn't help himself, just sat there shaking and sobbing in front of her on the stool. She left the sofa, wrapped an arm around him, gave him a tight squeeze. He couldn't remember the last time someone hugged him.

"It's okay," she said, tightening her grip. "It's okay." Eventually, she let go. "We'll talk more on Tuesday, right?" She straightened up. "And will you tell me more about those other gang members?" He nodded, meekly. "I'll ring Sue. Tell her you're willing to talk. It'll really help your cause, Robin. I can't stress that enough."

She let herself quietly out of the house.

He heard her car start up.

Shit.

He couldn't believe he'd got like that. What the fuck was wrong with him? He got to his feet, washed his face in the bathroom. Raked his hair back with a comb. This would be his last night. He *had* to get out of here. Start afresh someplace new, perhaps.

At a quarter to nine, he left his lodgings and headed for the village. Did he really want to do this? Not particularly. But he was going to get what he was owed. He needed the pills. Especially after that visit from the social worker. It had thrown him, leaving him anxious and afraid. He needed to block everything out. And fast.

It was getting dark. Pinprick stars glinted and trembled above. He passed a tractor with its engine running. Robin wondered if the driver was Jim, the customer from the pub yesterday. It was too dark to make out. Who cares, he immediately thought. He saw faint, flickering lights up on the hill. He thought about Dawn again; about how stupid he'd been for breaking down in front of her like that. Just because she'd mentioned his parents. What the fuck was wrong with him?

49

He noticed the sigils as he climbed the hill. Some were carved into the bark of trees, others scratched into rocks or in the earth beside his feet. He tried not to stop and think too much about what they might mean. Many of them matched the symbols often found engraved on the pills.

He saw the house as soon as he reached the top. It was in a bad way, missing sections of its roof and walls. He could see inside, discerning candlelight and people drifting and flitting. He approached a wide, doorless entrance, then slipped into a space lacking segregating walls and a ceiling. The stairs to his right led nowhere, rising before crumbling apart. There were candles everywhere. Flames jumped and sputtered. A dining table was positioned in the centre of the room, bare, unlaid. People milled about, laughing, chattering, many clutching flutes of champagne. Classical music played from speakers positioned in corners. There were strange and esoteric symbols painted on what remained of the walls.

The crowd was certainly an odd mix. There were youngsters and vagrant types, as well as elderly-looking guests dressed in tuxes, suits and ties. They mingled and interacted perfectly civilly, despite their different looks and backgrounds.

Someone tugged his sleeve. "Rob?"

Robin turned to see Charley, grinning at him.

"Hey," Charley said, "you made it! Let me get you a little something – stay there." He glanced around before raising and waving his hand to a waiter carrying a platter.

The waiter drifted over, staring vacantly at Robin who dropped his gaze. On the platter were glasses of champagne, lines of white powder and a plastic bowl filled with pills. He picked up one of the pills, casually tossing it into his mouth before swallowing.

"It'll be dinner soon," Charley explained. "Let me quickly introduce you to some of the others."

He led Robin by the arm to a small group of three youths, an elderly man and a large, middle-aged woman. Films of sweat seemed to cover the whole of their faces. He recognised the lad from the pub yesterday whose gaze, he felt, produced a vaguely threatening aura.

The elderly man addressed Robin in a loud, brash voice. "Our guest of honour!"

"Mr. Morgan looks after us," Charley explained.

"No, no, no," Mr. Morgan disagreed just as Robin remembered what was said about the man at the pub yesterday. "We look after *each other*, remember?" He grinned at Robin. "Wonderful to meet you, young man."

"Meet?" asked the woman and the youths kept their eyes locked on Robin and sniggered strangely at him. Charley broke away; Robin would have followed if his arm hadn't been grabbed.

"Dreadful business about the police," Mr. Morgan said.

Robin shook his arm free. "Sorry?"

"We have eyes everywhere, you know." He nodded over Robin's shoulder. Robin turned to see

Sue, the WPC, smiling at him, a flute glass of champagne raised in her right hand.

Robin felt his entire body turn to ice.

"Still," Mr. Morgan continued, "no harm done. At least we're finally up and not under this godforsaken hill anymore."

The middle-aged woman laughed and shook her head. "We're *free!* Raised up out of the ground from our prison in the earth. And we've grown so big and strong, because nearly everyone here has taken the oath." She looked pointedly at Robin. "Only the most devout can be a part of this, you know. But there are other ways we can flourish, expand and fill up the world."

Robin swallowed down his panic. "Excuse me," he said, breaking away, heading off quickly into the crowd. Guests in close proximity were now flinging open their arms, reading aloud from the runes painted on the walls. *What the fuck's going on here?* he thought. And where was Charley? He just wanted to get his pills and go now.

Candlelight and shadow flickered around him. Conversation gradually died away to be replaced by sinister chants and incantations.

He froze, noticing a couple kissing in a corner. Except, they weren't kissing – their faces were melded together, like they were Siamese or something.

His heart was thudding, pounding. Was the pill taking effect already? The weird stuff didn't usually happen this quickly.

Old man Morgan and the middle-aged woman shuffled forward, holding hands. Then, as they stepped away from each other, Robin saw their hands were still joined by a pink thread which surely couldn't be skin.

His gaze flashed everywhere. People were falling into one another, becoming shapeless and malformed. They were slipping in front of the crevices and apertures, barring all avenues of escape.

Charley was beside him now, gesturing to his sweat-soaked face. "We struggle when we separate. Feel worse the further we're apart."

Robin heard sighs of relief and groans of pleasure as the guests continued collapsing into each other. Robin realised old man Morgan's arms had disappeared into the flanks of two youths and ropes of flesh flickered and writhed at the top of his neck where his head should have been.

Robin screamed.

Suddenly he was grabbed by a vast array of hands, his body lifted, his feet quickly leaving the ground. He was marched over to the table, dumped unceremoniously onto it, a crowd of faces gathering to blot out the stars through the broken roof.

Robin slammed his eyes shut.

Just a nightmare, he thought. *Hallucinations brought on by the pill. They're not real, not real, not...*

Fingers clawed his eyes back open.

He saw the guests had merged into a single churning mass of mouths, limbs and eyes. A towering half-head formed, a long face projecting so many flickering features on it. Charley's grotesque grin slithered and weaved down that warping lump of bulging, contorted flesh.

Robin screamed at the top of his lungs, kicking and thrashing on the table.

"I want my Mum!" he shouted. "Dad! *Lucille!* I want them back! I want it how it used to be! Let me go! *LET ME...!*"

But the thing just laughed with its many mouths and reached out with its many hands, pulling, tearing him apart, stuffing chunks of him into its maws, ripping and devouring until Robin's screams had ceased and his silence was assured.

Consider the Prey

Rickey Rivers Jnr

Of all places to meet women, he met Nora inside of the mall restroom. There had been confusion on her part and she had entered the men's restroom and then quickly apologized to the only male there, David.

He was struck by her. She was tall and slender with dark lips and dark hair. She looked like a model. In fact David was sure that she must have been. She wore red high heels and a red and black dress. She seemed important. At least to David, she seemed more important than him.

When he left the restroom he found her standing outside the ladies room, adjusting her dress. For the first time in a long time he felt compelled to speak to a woman directly. A strange confidence rose within.

"Hello," he said, "funny situation."

The woman looked at him and smiled. Now David noticed her eyes. They were lovely and dark. She reminded him of someone out of a film noir.

"Yeah, I'm pretty absent minded," she said, pushing a strand of her hair behind her right ear.

"It's okay. I am too," said David.

They laughed.

He introduced himself, thought about extending his hand then rethought after thinking it weird to do so soon after leaving the restroom.

"I'm Nora," said the woman, extending her hand.

Now he felt dumb. He surrendered his and shook hers. Her nails dug into him.

"Sorry," she said. "I like my nails pretty long."

"Must be difficult to eat," he joked.

"Not when you use a knife and fork."

In return, he laughed. "Well, yeah." He thought of something. "What kind of food do you like?"

She smiled. "Well, pretty much anything."

"Me, I'm a vegetarian."

"So am I. I started last year. Sometimes I forget."

"Forget? Cheat meals?"

"Guilty. We all have them, right?" She laughed and David laughed. Truthfully, he didn't believe in cheat meals. He had been a strict vegetarian for years, but she didn't need to know that.

"So, David," she said. "Is that your way of asking me out?"

"Well I…" He thought about it. "You know what? Yes, I'm asking you on a date… is that okay?"

"Sure it is."

They exchanged numbers. Nora put a little smiley face beside hers.

"I guess I'll see you around," said David. He couldn't hide his boyish smile.

"Sure you will," said Nora. She wiggled her fingers at him and walked back into the main sector of the mall.

David stayed in the restroom hallway, staring down at Nora's number. He couldn't believe what just happened. He wondered what such a beautiful woman had been doing at the mall in this part of town. She didn't seem as if she belonged. It was more like she should have had security accompany her everywhere. Maybe she would have if this had been Hollywood. He thought that she'd be a better fit there.

He had found talking to her was easy. But why had it been so easy? And why did he care? Because worrying was familiar, something he had picked up from his mom. It was healthy after all, a natural thing. But why worry over something so simple? Why did worrying feel like the right state of mind sometimes? And was it even worry? Or was it instead paranoia? What was the difference?

During times of pressure a childhood figure came to mind, a cartoon character named Captain Courage. He fought off attacks from all sides of his mind and anxiety took on a ghoulish form.

After this chance encounter something strange happened with time. It seemed to accelerate.

***

It took David days to finally call Nora. Captain Courage had hounded him about it. During this time he didn't sleep well, partly due to nervous thoughts of meeting Nora again and partly due to dreams that seemed to recur. Bad dreams weren't new to him, like any other person he got them sporadically. But these dreams had been different.

One in particular stuck with him. It started outdoors in the middle of nowhere. A street isolated in a void. Children were playing with a red ball on a circular street. The sky was dark and swirling grey. Soon the ball strayed and fell onto a nearby circular platform, independent of their play area. In fact, David hadn't noticed the platform until the ball landed there.

The boys stood on the edge of the street while the ball waited on the platform. There was a space between the two areas. Surely it would pull you into the void. One of the boys volunteered to fetch the ball. He leapt from the street and floated onto the other platform. The other boys cheered visibly, not audibly. The boy went towards the ball and noticed that the platform had a pattern on it. It looked like a pentagram. The entire platform had been that. The ball waited in the middle of it. The boy reached for the ball but found his feet bound where he stood. In the distance the boy saw a figure with fleshy wings approach from the sky, then swoop down for him. With its bird-like talons the figure grabbed the boy and flew away.

Somehow this dream had compelled David to call Nora, more so than the hero in his head. Mostly he didn't want to be alone with his thoughts, but he also didn't want to accidentally fall asleep and repeat the dream. It had scared him.

When he woke up he would push his fingernails into his fingertips to ensure he was actually awake. Sometimes this didn't help and he couldn't feel the pain. Those times frightened him the most because he knew the dreams weren't finished with him. Those times made his heart race. He felt the date would clear his head. He wanted to see Nora. He felt that he had to. Something inside him saidt seeing her would help. Being with another person would be healthier than staying home alone.

And so Nora and David set up a date that was soon cancelled and then rescheduled to take place at Nora's home. He was to meet her tonight and the anxiety over this hit him harder as time went on. During the entire car ride to Nora's house he practiced his breathing exercises, opting not to take his pills. They had side effects. Side effects he didn't want to deal with around her.

Soon David stood at Nora's door and waited before knocking.

"Calm down," he told himself. "You're okay, you're okay."

Why had he been so afraid? Something in the back of his mind was telling him to run to his car and never call again. But that hadn't been her fault. She was an innocent party. He couldn't blame this woman for bad dreams. Why should nightmares hinder him from living his life? Why should anxiety stop him from doing anything?

He was strong, he was brave. There wasn't anything to be afraid of. Superheroes don't get scared. His hand throbbed. He looked down and saw Nora's nail marks. An inside voice motivated, hushed his cowardice.

He pulled in a big breath, held it and then let it go. He knocked on Nora's door.

"Would you like some wine?"

"No thanks, I don't drink."

"Sure you do." Nora had already taken the wine glasses from her kitchen cabinet and put them on the coffee table, all the time keeping her eyes on him. He felt compelled to look away, but found it difficult to do.

Nora fetched a bottle of red wine, removed the cork and poured half glasses for both of them. She sat next to him on the couch with her eyes still on him and his on hers. She reached for her glass and motioned for him to do the same. He did. A sweet aroma arose from the glass. They drank. For him the wine went down syrupy and thick. It slid down his throat like sludge. He coughed, finally breaking her gaze.

"What kind of wine is this?"

"Red wine."

"Well, it's red but-"

"You've never had wine before, have you?"

How did she know that? "No," he said.

"I see you haven't."

He felt small, immature. Thick wine seemed peculiar, but he felt he shouldn't question it. He felt himself dumb for questioning her. She knew more about alcohol than him, since he knew nothing about alcohol at all. Besides, he had always wondered what wine would taste like. He didn't expect it to be thick. Was this the case for all alcohol? He remembered his father drinking beer and friends from school drinking the same brand

and trying to get him to drink too. He never did. What was the name of the brand?

"You like it?" she asked, pursing her lips.

"Oh, I like it," he said. A lie, would she buy it?

"No, you don't." She laughed.

David smiled an awkward smile then laughed in the same manner. He felt anxiety creeping. He was uncomfortable here. He couldn't trust himself drunk, so he set down his glass, though all the wine was gone from it. Apparently, he had finished it. The beer brand came back to back to him, it made him smile goofy.

The hero inside stumbled.

His hand throbbed.

"Feel free to have more," said Nora with a giggle.

"Oh no, I'm fine, really."

***

Seeing Nora cut into her steak had made him sick. He wanted to say that but he kept his composure. Furthermore, he felt the alcohol kick in, really kick in. He was woozy.

"Really, a wonderful thing," said Nora.

Apparently she had been talking, but what about?

"I like the fair," she continued.

The fair, they were talking about the fair for some reason. Had he brought that up? Had he spoke of taking her to the fair? Why couldn't he remember?

"Cotton candy," she said and then what felt like seconds later, "ferris wheels are romantic."

"Yes," he said, not knowing why, just agreeing, felt grown up to just nod and smile.

"Clowns are fun too, but some people don't like them." Nora was holding a conversation with herself, directed towards him. He didn't know when the conversation started or when they went from the couch to the kitchen table. What happened to lost time? Why was she talking about the fair and, more importantly, why had she been eating a steak? His mind just picked up on it. It didn't make sense. Hadn't she been a vegetarian? Wasn't he? He took a look down at his plate. There was a steak there, it looked rare. The red, red meat stared back at him. Why was he eating steak? His mouth was wet, but it didn't taste like meat. He felt sick. No, he needed to clear his head. He made up a lie.

"Nora," he said, interrupting her.

"Yes," she said, showing no signs of annoyance. Like she knew his actions before he did them.

"I have to, m-may…" He trailed, pulled in some breath through his nose. "May I use your bathroom?"

Nora nodded. "Sure."

His tongue felt weird in his mouth. Asking her the question had been difficult. His mouth was full of saliva. He didn't feel hungry, but all the same he salivated. He stood up from the table and walked away. It felt like he had too many feet. He turned and asked her where the bathroom was.

"Down the hall," she said, "to your right."

He nodded and went in that direction. He looked around, disoriented as he walked down the hall. The hallway seemed small and tight as if you couldn't fully extend your arms there. He tried doing so. No, for sure you couldn't. The hallway seemed specifically made for Nora, the ceiling high and the sides pulled in, perfect for a tall and slim person.

He reached the end of the hall and saw the bathroom door. He grabbed the door handle. Something compelled him to turn his attention to the door behind him. He felt an urge to go there, but in some way he didn't want to. A strange sweat developed on the nape of his neck. He made his choice and left the lie of the bathroom behind him.

He walked into this unwelcome room and felt around for a light switch. The room was dark, but not so dark he couldn't see. Then he forgot about the light switch. On one side of the room he saw a washer and a dryer. On the other side a sink and in front of him a shelf. *A laundry room,* he thought, *normal enough.*

He started to leave, but couldn't take his eyes away from the shelf. He walked forward and saw that it had been full of bottles, some of them with liquid in them. He thought to himself, *she keeps her wine in the laundry room, that's funny.* But he couldn't laugh. The humor didn't seem funny in that way, but funny in a way that made him uneasy, funny in a way that didn't make sense. *Why would the wine be here? Is this normal?*

He felt nauseous. Now he really was sick, he turned to go to the bathroom. As soon as that thought came to mind the laundry room door closed and the room went dark and quiet. He swallowed so hard it hurt. Where was his confidence wing man? Where was Captain Courage? He could feel a presence with him, but it was impossible to see in the blackness. Something or someone was there, but why had their shape been hidden? He stood stiff against the shelf and waited for something to happen, whoever or whatever didn't seem to move.

He wanted to say Nora's name, but his lips quivered and the room felt colder, oppressive. He tried to focus his eyes in the dark, but he couldn't make out a figure no matter how hard he tried. His saliva dripped from his mouth and onto his shirt. He didn't bother wiping it. Behind him the bottles shook from on the shelf. They made unusual sounds like something was in them, reaching out to him. The pain in his hand came back. He felt warm breath on his throat and chest.

Internally he said a small prayer. He tried to say her name, but it came out as a stutter. He didn't feel very super. He felt very David, very human and plain. He could not move his legs. They were frozen. He'd somehow been paralyzed by the darkness and lack of vision, somehow paralyzed by something. Come on, he told himself, jump out of my head and save me. But Captain Courage wasn't there, no one was there but fear. The thought that even superheroes die had now become cruelly apparent to him.

Superheroes were supposed to swoop in and save the weak. They were supposed to be protectors. But David didn't have a protector. He didn't have anything but himself. Superheroes were fiction, reality was different.

In reality, what else could fly? What else flew? The winged thing with the boy in the dream, surely that couldn't be true.

He pressed his fingernails against his fingertips. He could feel that. He could also feel the throb in his hand.

"I'm here," she said.

Something sharp went into him. He was lifted. The sky was dark and swirling grey.

Random Thoughts

Dorothy Davies

It's boring lying here, nothing to do but think. I started dwelling on that silly old song about the worms that crawl in and out, how they crawl in thin and crawl out stout – and I started thinking about worms, cans of worms.

So tell me, whoever is listening, what is it with the 'can of worms' metaphor?

My questions are as follows:

Who thought up the idea of putting worms in a can?

Why did anyone think it was a good idea to put worms in a can?

How did they collect the worms to go into the can?

How many worms can you get in a can?

How many cans of worms did they think they could sell?

Did they think others would want to buy/eat the worms?

What do worms taste like?

How much is a can of worms…

There are just so many questions you can ask without getting answers – there are no answers, so I must switch my questions.

Someone said the dead had no need of blood.

My question here is – what happens to those who do?

You see, I do…

And I want out of here before the damn worms come crawling.

Anyone want to give me a hand to get out of here?

No reward, just the thrill of doing a good deed for the day. There aren't enough zombies in the world; the world is in desperate need of another one.

Me.

Monster on My Street

Rickey Rivers Jr.

In this neighborhood the sun shined bright. All the lawns were perfectly cut, edged and symmetrical. All the mail boxes stood straight and fine. All the houses were in order. Hedges perfectly shaped, trees perfectly trimmed, and sidewalks clear of debris. Clean gutters, clean streets, everything clean and quiet.

A young girl sat in her front yard, playing with toys, doing voices for the characters. This was a normal. Everything was as it should be. The sterile place was quite a happy indeed. Was, because a car cruised onto her street and soon pulled in front of her home. The driver's side window rolled down and a man spoke from inside.

"Hello."

The girl looked up from her toys and smiled at the man.

"Are your parents home?" asked the man.

The girl shook her head.

The man stepped out of his car and walked across the finely cut grass. He wore sandals, long shorts and a coat. His hair was like the cheese of a pizza. Somehow his sunglasses were balanced on his slippery looking forehead. Beyond his dark coat the girl saw a stain on his undershirt.

"Yellow," she said to herself.

The man stood over the girl with a smile on his face. "What you doing?"

"Playing," said the girl.

"I see," said the man. "Nice toys."

"Thanks." The girl introduced her toys by name and held up each to show him. "This is Tabitha, this is Cheryl, this is Monica and this is Mr. Sniffles." The toys were: a blonde doll, a brown haired doll, a dark haired doll and a stuffed animal (cat). "I have more inside."

"Hello everyone," said the man.

The girl said hello in different voices for each doll and meowed for the stuffed animal.

The man chuckled. "And what's your name?"

"Can't tell you."

"Why is that?"

"I'm not supposed to talk to strangers."

"Hey, I'm not a stranger. My name's Jim."

"Okay, Jim. I don't know you."

"Well, you can get to know me if you come with me."

He gestured towards his car, a sleek powder white four door with dark windows. From what the girl could see the car had no blemishes. Unlike the man, the exterior was clean.

"No thank you," said the girl. "I'm satisfied here."

"You can be more satisfied with me," said the man, putting a hand over his front. He touched himself then stopped once he realized that she would not look at him further.

"How old are you?" asked the man.

"Not old enough," said the girl.

"I think you are." He lowered his voice. "I want you to get into my car. You can take your toys with you."

The girl looked up at him. She studied his face. Then she stood.

"Oh, you're one of those." She was at the height of his belt buckle. "You must not have heard about me."

"Heard about you? Are you famous?"

"No, silly."

"Well then," the man reached into his coat pocket, revealing a small gun. "Do as I say."

"Wow, a gun," said the girl.

"It works too."

"I'm sure."

"I don't want to disturb this nice neighborhood but if I have to, I will."

"You won't disturb anyone," said the girl. "And you won't shoot me."

"I won't?" He pointed the gun directly at her. The girl didn't budge.

"I'm serious," said the man.

"Put your gun in my mouth," said the girl.

"Oh? Is that foreplay?" He laughed. "Naughty, I see. I knew from the moment I saw you." He grinned, showing his teeth, crooked, his smile wide, skin crinkling at the cheeks.

"Please, put your gun into my mouth," said the girl, her expression stoic, her tone enthused.

The man took a step forward. The girl opened her mouth and the man slid the barrel in, slow.

"So, is this some type of fetish for you?" He ran his tongue over his lips and grabbed at his crotch. "It's working for me."

In an instant the girl chomped down and bit off the gun tip.

The man's eyes bulged and his lips quivered. The slippery word "what?" could almost be heard from him. The vibration from the bite shook his hand up to his arm and shoulder. It was as though electricity had shaken him and rattled his mind. The hairs on his neck stood like his extremity would and the tingle below became uncomfortable.

The girl chewed the metal and swallowed. Then she opened her mouth and stuck out her tongue.

"All gone."

The man looked at his useless gun, then at the girl then back at the gun.

"Now," said the girl. "Imagine what else I can do."

The man's mouth hung open. He took a step back. The fear inside reflected and was shown back to him via the mirror of her eyes. He mouthed something and blinked. He couldn't think. He re-aimed what was left of his gun and fired a shot.

The girl stood there.

When the man realized that the gun had blowback, he screamed and cursed and dropped the remains of the weapon. He ran back to his car holding his bloody used-to-be hand, at the same time painting the white driver's door red.

The girl watched him drive one handed and clumsily crash into a tree down the street.

"Wow," said the girl, watching the bloody man escape from the car, drag his body along the ground and yell for help.

"He might survive," she said to no one.

The car exploded and set the man ablaze.

"He still might be okay." She noticed the half chewed gun on the grass. "Wonderful, he left a snack." She picked it up and bit into it. She took her time chewing, watching as the burning body crawled, rolled and then finally curled into a ball.

"Good snack, bad man," said the girl and went back to her toys. She noticed the blood on Mr. Sniffles and licked him clean like a mother cat would.

Someone somewhere distant must have called the police, because soon a police car arrived, blaring its siren. She hated the sound.

The siren stopped and a man left his car. He ran to his trunk and fetched a fire extinguisher. He cooled off the body and then tended to the burning car and finally the burning tree the car ran into. He cursed a few times and surveyed the neighborhood. He saw her sitting there on her lawn and she saw him too. She waved. The officer ran in her direction so she stood to greet him.

"Hey," he called upon reaching her lawn. "Did you see what happened?"

"Oh yes," said the girl. She told him about the crash with scant details.

"Must have been a drunk driver," the officer said to himself, not noticing the red beneath him.

"No," said the girl. "He wasn't drunk."

"He wasn't? Wait, he spoke to you?"

"Yes, and he pointed a gun at me."

"A gun? Where is it?" He looked around, seeing the wet red lawn.

"I ate it."

"...what?"

"I ate his gun and it was good."

"You ate evidence? His fingerprints could have...you're not supposed to..." The officer shook his head.

"Is something wrong?" asked the girl.

"Don't do that again!" said the officer, raising his voice.

"Don't speak to me that way," she said, her tone the same.

"Um, please don't do that again."

"I'll try not to."

"Good, that's real good," the officer swallowed. His throat suddenly dry, the back of his neck warm and wet.

"Don't be scared, Mr. Police Officer. You're good," said the girl.

He stuttered, "That's right, police officers are good. We're the good guys."

"I know that. Yes, I do."

"Yeah, yeah, we're good."

"If you're good then stay good, yes?"

"Yes, I will."

"Be a good man."

"I will, I will," he over smiled, showing his teeth, his eyes revealing the truth inside.

"And if you do, you'll have nothing to worry about."

"Yes, yes of course. This-a, the neighborhood looks nice. Everything in order, I see."

"Always is."

"Yeah, that's good. I'm sorry I have to-to attend to-"

"The bad man."

"Yes, I have to do my job," said the man, the fear squeezing him, a python grip.

"Okay, goodbye," said the girl, a smile on her face.

The policeman left her standing there and hurried to attend to the corpse. Then he called in the scene, asking for ambulance and fire rescue assistance. He tried his best to remain calm. The girl read his lips the whole time.

"I wish he didn't crash that car," she said. "It was much nicer than him."

Birds chirped in nearby trees. A squirrel skittered across a rooftop and the wind blew nice and cool. Eventually, the smoke dissipated.

The drippings of a man soaked into the freshly cut lawn. Soon, the neighborhood returned to normal. Even the smell of the air returned, no longer made foul by the stench of a stranger. And what was that smell? Pine, summer freshness, grass clippings, newness, this smell rose into the air and settled upon the neighborhood, refreshing it, as if poured from a jar.

The girl resumed play with more voices for the toys. Try as she might, she could not get them to sound as they once had before though her cat's meow had improved considerably.

And the Rest Is Silence

Rie Sheridan Rose

It started with silence. Eerie silence against a cold, gray dawn. No streaks of red and gold broke through the heavy cloud cover. I might have been alone on the streets. Odd for a Monday. The traffic was negligible—almost non-existent. Also odd for a Monday.

I shared the world with the silence. And the vultures.

They hulked atop the lampposts, black silhouettes against the pearl-gray sky. Maybe they were buzzards... but vultures is so much more descriptive and who is there now to care if I misidentify one of God's creatures? He certainly seems to have turned a blind eye on the world below His heavenly realm.

Monday morning and I made it to work in ten minutes. That's usually a thirty minute drive with the traffic. To park my car on the first floor of the garage was another treat but the vultures watching silently from the street lights took the edge off the pleasure.

I hurried into the building as fast as I could, one eye on the brooding birds. It was a relief to get inside. I know vultures and buzzards don't usually attack the living... but seeing a committee in session is unsettling.

I got to my desk without seeing another living soul. Normally Virginia would have been at the reception desk well before I made it in. Parker would be on the telephone arguing with a customer over some change he didn't want to implement— he'd never gotten the hang of "the customer is always right," no matter how many times we tried to drum it into his thick skull.

At the very least Matthew would beat me in. He practically lived in his office, struggling with all the duties it takes to manage a start-up. But his light was off and the room was empty.

Maybe I'd missed a memo. Was it a holiday or something? I checked the calendar and no, it wasn't a scheduled day off. Maybe someone had called an informal hookey holiday and decided not to invite me. But that didn't explain the traffic... and it seemed hardly likely Matt would have signed off on such a thing. We were supposed to make a presentation on Friday. This made it all the more disturbing that there was no one here.

I had been working my ass off, but my part wasn't ready to go—I didn't see how Parker could be done with his. Still, the silence was good for one thing. It was easier to focus without all the normal distractions of a typical day at the office. I figured out the blocker to my progress and by the end of the workday, I was in much better shape than I had been.

Not a single person came in all day.

Not a single phone rang.

Not a single IM pinged across my chat screen.

It was as if the world had ended—like the Twilight Zone episode where Burgess Meredith is the last man on Earth and now he has time to read all the books he can find... until he breaks his glasses. Perhaps I was in the same predicament and no one had let me know the news. At least I didn't wear glasses.

On my way back to the garage, I glanced up, looking for the vultures. Even those silent sentinels had deserted me.

I threw my briefcase in the passenger seat, then got behind the wheel and pushed the button for the radio. Surely there would be some news story or something. It had been at least eight hours since I'd heard another voice.

There was only silence... and a vague static if I turned the volume up as high as it would go. I didn't leave it there—when the sound came back, I didn't want to be startled off the road by the blast of noise.

I needed sound.

The tires screeched a little as I whipped out of the garage and it was curiously comforting. That was what tires were supposed to do under duress. I felt a little better.

That comfort soon died away again, however, as I drove to the heart of town. I craved people and noise. Music. Horns honking. Street corner hustlers. Anything!

Nothing.

The restaurants were closed and empty. The neon was dark. The corners were vacant.

No hordes of shambling zombies... but no people either. No little piles of ash from the Rapture. No Mother-ships hovering overhead.

Only me, my car and the silence.

And the vultures, back to brooding on the lampposts.

I was irrationally pleased to see them. At least I wasn't completely alone.

That was three months ago. There's plenty of food and water; the electrical grid is up for the environmental necessities; the vultures seem to be doing fine. But there's no sound. Even my DvD player refuses to cooperate.

I've started naming the vultures, my only companions. I wonder if you can teach them to speak...?

Hemogoblin

Chris Rodriguez

Bennie's back creaked as she bent to pick up the mousetrap, followed by deep lines creasing her forehead. The bait hadn't been touched. She'd tried cheese and peanut butter. Her sister told her to try bacon. It would take a full slice to bait all the traps around the house. *Lord knows I could go without bacon for one meal.*

"I don't know what else to do, Sher. I can hear it rattling around in the cupboards at night. The unholy racket wakes me up. Lord knows it takes a lot to wake *me* from a sound sleep."

"How do you know it's a mouse, Bennie? Might be a rat if it's that noisy."

"You would know better than me, Sher," Bennie told her sister. "Lord knows how many varmints you all catch out on the homestead. I'll go get some bigger traps this afternoon. I can't take much more."

Artie scanned the traps, then stood looking at them as if he was calculating an engineering project. "You sure it's a rat? I ain't never heard of no rat doing all the things you say this one is."

"I'm not sure, Artie. That's the problem. I can hear it. I can see the damage it's doing. I just haven't seen the dang critter itself."

"What about leavings? Can't you see any signs? You know, like... poops?"

Bennie ran the question through the rat maze in her brain before answering. "Yes, but I'm not sure how to explain it. Black and tarry. It's the devil to clean up - smeared all over everything!

Artie shrugged, lost for an explanation.

"Can I post this flyer?" Bennie showed him the photo of her cat. Shoofly disappeared a few days after this critter showed up. She could hear him growling at the thing as he skittered around trying to flush it out. One night he outright screamed and bolted through the kittie door, never to be seen again. He must have got bitten, though. A trail of blood spots went all the way to the back fence.

"If you can find a spot, you're welcome to it." He turned to point at the multitude of missing pet posters in the window. "Don't know what's happening with everyone's animals this week. Kinda weird if ya ask me."

It took a couple of hours to clear the cupboards, clean up and disinfect the sticky mess left behind. It was getting hot so she made a pitcher of iced tea and brought out cookies in the tin for the afternoon visit with her best friend.

Mary-Madeline listened to Bennie's problem and poured herself another glass of tea. "When I was a girl, I heard tell of critters like that in our town." She added an extra spoonful of sugar as if it would help erase the bitter childhood memories. "Old Mammy, she told us the town was cursed, infested with evil sprites, goblins or some such things. They had blood-red eyes and raised holy hell

80

in everyone's households, killed pets, bit off children's fingers."

"Lord knows you've been my friend for a long time, Mary-Madeline, but you sure do come up with some stories. Tallest tales I ever heard."

"All I know is it lasted through the fall until the tent preacher came and called the whole community together to pray for days. I don't know what was more terrifying, my brother, the out-of-control creatures or the hell-and-damnation meetings. People were moaning, dropping to the floor in fits, speaking in strange tongues. I dunno." Mary-Madeline rocked violently in the chair as if she expected to be carried away from the uncomfortable recollection.

Toward evening, Bennie baited the new traps and set them near the places she had cleaned the most. She was distracted by Mary-Madeline's stories from her hometown far away. *I doubt anything like that could happen these days*. A sharp pain brought her back to the present in a flash.

Her finger, pricked by a small wire on the trap, was bleeding freely from a puncture. She sucked on it to staunch the flow as she shoved the trap gingerly with her toe between the stove and refrigerator. She noticed blood spattered on the bacon bait, but shrugged it off. *Lord knows it'll add a little flavor. Couldn't hurt.*

Bennie woke in the night. Why? The house was quiet for the first time in a long while. Maybe the sound of the SNAP! had awakened her.

The blankets on her bed fluttered. "Shoofly? Is it you, Puss-Puss?" She pushed up on her elbows just as the covers flew off the bed. Startled, she reached for her glasses. "Ouch!" She yanked her hand back and squinted at it in the dark. A heavy pulse pounded in her neck. Something was terribly wrong. Car headlights swept the room just in time for her to see something that defied logic, the finger she had pricked earlier was gone. Her mind pinwheeled. "Lord, Lord! What's happening?"

More car lights revealed the grotesque figure of a creature standing on her bed. Terror in her eyes registered what she saw, but her brain rejected it. Hell's demons had somehow found their way into her bedroom. One stood on the nightstand beside her bed; a foot high with scaly spikes and long needle-sharp teeth. The red eyes were what left the biggest impression on Bennie. *Goblins!*

Another scream built up in her throat as the pair leapt onto her chest. The overpowering smell of sulfur and ammonia burned the breath from her lungs. Warm blood splattered onto her face before her throat disintegrated under the saw blades in their mouths.

This time the bait worked.

Embolus

Edmund Stone

Johnny stepped out of the bar onto Bourbon Street into the balmy evening. He needed a place to think. The bench by the river would be good, no tourists this time of night. A voice spoke to him from the shadows in hushed tones.

"Hey. You, man. You got problems, don't you?"

Johnny stopped and a woman stepped in front of him. Her form was only partially visible in the faint light of a corner streetlamp. Johnny could see she had a skull painted on her forehead and a few symbols on her cheeks. The white paint was a stark contrast to her dark skin.

"Who are you?"

She said, "I'm the answer to your prayers," in a thick Cajun accent. She was holding a bottle in her hand. It looked old, like the ones in an ancient apothecary shop. "Dis here I'm a-holding has the power to rid you of the demon floating in your blood. This'll take care of it."

"You know about my medical condition?"

"Of course, the black death of cancer's written all over you. For twenty dollars, I'm gonna give you the cure. Ain't no doctors know about this one, I can assure you. Keep you from takin' the filthy poison they gives."

"Naw, I'm good," he said and turned to walk away.

"You thinkin' you better than me?" the woman scoffed. "Those doctors got you fixed and all healed now? How's all it workin' out for ya?"

He thought about her words and how his condition, if not treated properly, could kill him. But the treatment wasn't much better than the disease itself. Chemo probably. The assurance of more pain. Maybe she was right. He reached in his pocket and pulled a twenty from his wallet. She eagerly took it and handed over the potion.

"Drink it as soon as possible," she said, then produced a knife.

Johnny stepped away from her, unsure what she was proposing. She turned the handle toward him.

"Here. You'll need this as well." Then she disappeared into the darkness before he could ask why.

Johnny put the knife inside his jacket and walked on until he reached the bench. He sat, lit a cigarette and considered the small bottle. The liquid was black and clung to the sides when he turned it in his hand. It seemed his life had been stultified by recent events and if this little potion gave even a partial bit of relief, it'd be worth it. He uncapped the bottle and turned up the contents, drinking it in one gulp. The taste was bitter at first, then had a sweeter aftertaste. Something like licorice, he thought.

Nothing happened. Frustrated, he slung the bottle into the river, took a deep breath and stared at the waning moon in the sky. He took one last draw from the cigarette and threw it on the sidewalk, crushing it with his foot. Johnny stood, stretched and yawned. He was ready to go home. But when he stepped forward, he felt the world spinning around him. He sat to get his bearings. Something was moving in his body, working its way from his head and down into the rest of his limbs. Finally, it landed in his gut. He had the sensation of being full, like he'd eaten a very large meal. His gut continued to swell, pushing against the buttons of his shirt. Nausea overtook him and he fell to his knees, retching, as the contents of his stomach were released onto the sidewalk in front of him.

The sour taste of vomitous burned his throat and mouth but he was relieved to have it out. In front of him lay a gelatinous mass of bloody excrement. It was crusty on the edges. Like a scab falling from a wound. Shockingly, it began creeping toward him.

Johnny stumbled backward, trying to scramble away but it picked up speed. He got to his feet and took off in a dead run, but there was no escape. The bloody mass knocked him down; his arms splayed out before him. It lay on his back, digging for purchase, trying to consume him. Johnny wriggled to his side, attempting to free himself of the creature, but it only dug deeper. He felt his clothing rip. The thing meant to tear him apart.

He fought with it, his hands digging into the pulp, but he couldn't grab anything to help push the monster from him. Excrement oozed in a sticky mess down his arms and he fought the urge to vomit again. His hands ventured deeper into the creature until he hit something inside. It felt solid. Johnny squeezed and the thing shuddered but continued the onslaught with renewed fury. It wrapped around his body, covering him until only his head remained showing. It was then Johnny remembered the knife in his jacket pocket.

His arms burned from the creature touching his skin, but he ignored it and moved his hand toward the jacket until he retrieved the weapon. He grabbed the handle and thrust it in the middle of the monster, hitting the solid area. The creature immediately began to retreat, rolling from him. It tried to slink away but Johnny wouldn't let it. He thrust the knife again and again until it no longer moved. He wiped the excrement from his hands and watched the bloody mass ooze down the steps and into the river.

Johnny reached for a cigarette but pulled a crusty piece of blood back instead. He threw it to one side. Probably needed to quit anyway. He turned for home, already feeling better.

Epistaxis

E. S. Sibbald

There's blood on the sink, running slowly toward the drain, painting abstract starbursts, stark against the white porcelain. Droplets on the floor, a wet breadcrumb trail leading from my bedroom, down the hall and into the bathroom. Red spots on the mirror like sea spray.

The tissues pressed to my nose grow damp too quickly. I gather a thick wad in my other hand and quickly swap them. A drip escapes, splatting on the bench like a teardrop.

My eyelids are heavy and my head feels clouded with fog. The blood shows no sign of slowing and I fear if it doesn't soon, I will pass out.

The tissues are soaked through again, my fingertips wet with blood. I keep pinching the end of my nose and, with no other escape, the blood spills backward down my throat. It floods my mouth like thick, metallic bile. I spit into the sink. Mixed with my saliva, it becomes a thick red goop.

It feels like drowning. I inhale deeply through my nose and only realise my mistake when it's too late. The blood flooding my nose is drawn back and something thick and wet hits the back of my throat. I retch and push it forward into my mouth. It feels like jelly, only twice as slippery and thin around the edges like it's melting.

I spit violently; the clot slides down my tongue and into the basin with a wet splat. It moves lazily, leaving a shiny, pinkish trail in its wake.

I hadn't even noticed the persistent rush from my nose had become a dribble, turned off like a tap as suddenly as it had begun. I was distracted by my disgust over *that* coming out of my mouth. Slowly and carefully, so as not to set it off again, I begin to move the wet wad of tissues.

Red is smeared all over my face; smudges circling my nostrils, up the bridge of my nose, cracked lines where it had dripped down my lips and chin, even scattered along one cheekbone like a constellation of freckles.

Something tugs inside my nose as if a rope is drawn tight from the tissue to the back of my brain. I can feel it behind my eyes. It feels odd and vaguely painful, a sensation somewhere between pinching and tickling.

A dark, heavy, gummy string is stuck to the tissues, stretching up into my nose. With each tug further from my face, I can feel it rub against the canal of my nostril.

My hand is four inches from my nose and still the clot is stuck. The feeling of it endlessly sliding through my nose is making me gag. A traitorously pessimistic part of my brain tells me that it's acting as a plug and the moment I pull it out, the blood will come rushing and the whole ordeal will start over again – but I can't just leave it hanging there. I pull and pull and pull. The tail end comes out with one final ferocious tug.

Blood instantly begins to spill from my nose again, dribbling down my neck and onto my shirt. It draws warm trails all over my skin, but I don't reach for the tissues. The stream of blood doesn't seem so important anymore.

The thing that came out of my nose is curled up in the sink. It's the length of my forearm and thick as a garden hose. It's slick black where the blood is running off its glossy body and it's *moving*.

I gasp and when the thing turns to look at me, exposing tiny, jagged teeth running around a circular jaw, the gasp morphs into a scream.

The creature leaps, its open maw coming straight towards me. For an instant I can imagine it latching onto my nose, slicing easily through my soft meat with those many teeth, but it doesn't. It slides into my open screaming mouth.

Instinctively I wrench my jaw shut, but I'm too slow. My teeth sink into thick squishy flesh. The creature lets out a high-pitched squeal in response. I can feel the cry scrape through my body, clawing at my bones and tugging at my nerves.

It hits the back of my throat and I choke. I can't breathe. This thing is going to kill me. Its body tenses up like a tightly coiled spring and then, with one final push, it slips down my throat. Seconds later, I feel it hit my stomach.

It stops moving.

I could convince myself none of this had been real, that I had imagined it, a delusion from the blood loss if I couldn't still feel the creature pressed heavy against my organs.

I look at my reflection in the mirror. My nose has stopped bleeding.

Silver

Rickey Rivers Jr.

The evening sun warms the deep forest. Here you will find a single cabin. Inside you will find the man, doing what he does. From a distance you can hear the clanging, get closer and you will see the shadow, large, moving on the inside walls. Even in these times, when a blacksmith was thought to be unneeded, a good blacksmith would always find work.

One time he had been requested to forge a shield for a lowly knight. This shield needed to be light yet thick enough to withstand the breath of a great dragon. And the blacksmith did forge that shield and the shield was indeed strong. The knight had been thankful and paid the blacksmith handsomely.

Another time a young woman had come to him in need of a dagger. This woman did not have much money but the blacksmith, perhaps feeling pity (the woman looked to be abused), obliged and was able to fashion a thin iron dagger. When the same young woman later married into a royal family, she returned to the blacksmith and paid him more than enough for his effort. For this, he was thankful.

The blacksmith cared not what the weapons were for, he made them to live and this was, for him, an honorable profession. To some, this skill

91

was only that, a petty skill. But for the blacksmith, this skill embodied life itself. Without it, he could not imagine himself doing anything else, at least not with enthusiasm.

His profession was a useful one and he, a trustworthy man. So this time, when his current task had been proposed to him by a costumer with not much to offer, he hesitated, but then he remembered the young woman from before and accepted the job cautiously. To better this deal the costumer, a family man, had donated a bag of coal for the blacksmith's fire and the blacksmith did appreciate the barter.

Though thankful, the blacksmith warned that the weapon would not be of high grade, it could not be so. The weapon would not be practical for combat. In response, the family man had said that the weapon didn't need to be high grade. It would be for a stationary target, it needed only to be sharp.

The family man wanted a silver sword, not for fighting but for killing. The blacksmith did not argue. It would be easier to make a weapon that was only for flesh and would not need to pierce armor or break shield. It would not take him long to complete this task.

The family man handed him a slip of paper. On it, the name of the man who would retrieve the weapon in one week's time. The deed, the kill, was to be done by a third party, unknown to the blacksmith but known to the family man. Of course, this information meant nothing to the blacksmith.

Almost immediately after materials were gathered, the blacksmith began his work. For days he worked on the weapon, hammering, searing, grinding, bending, melting, and sharpening.

In past times, with larger amounts, the blacksmith could engrave a name on the sword or, if wanted, a symbol. But in making this sword, he had to remind himself of the weapon's purpose.

In some moments he thought of who the weapon might be for but he hushed himself, it was not business that mattered to him. In fact, it was dangerous for a blacksmith to get involved in the business of others. He had to remain unbiased and open to forge for any and all who approached, without judgement. After all, the money would spend the same. Who was he to judge? Who was he to care?

Over time, after days of labor, the sword was formed. It sat in the cabin, oh how it shone, and he was satisfied with his work. Now he need only wait for the sword retriever.

From the viewpoint of his oak chair he eyed the weapon. The sword reflected the light of his fire pit, a beautiful sight. He was proud of this blade but soon it would leave him, like all his forgings. And then, once more, he would be alone, cleaning his work space and waiting for a visitor.

***

Somewhere off yonder you will find a field, near a barn. Near the barn a farmhouse, inside this farmhouse lived a family. Presently, this family were all in the same room. The father standing, worried and mumbling, the mother sitting, angry and bothered and the son, lying on the bed between them, asleep. There was a silence in the farmhouse, in the room, but the minds of two wandered.

The father, blaming himself, thinking of the incident, him trying to protect his son but not being able to, the mother, angry with her husband, blaming him, even for things she knew he could not have prevented. Truthfully, neither parent could blame themselves.

The incident: the mother did not understand the nature, all she knew was that on that night her husband had carried their son across a field and her son had been exhausted and bloody. Secretly, her husband had taken him and cleaned him and laid him to rest. She knew that her husband was not telling her the whole truth, only a version. She knew that he had been trying to protect her but she also knew that her son could not be blamed for his actions. The boy had been passed out in a field, naked, around him, slain cattle, his doing. The image of that night had stuck with the father.

In some ways, the mother resented her husband, though she understood resentment was foolish. She did not have anyone else to blame and she for sure would not blame her son, her only child, for he could not help what he became.

Once before, a home doctor had come and tried to diagnose the boy (vitals and such) but the child had tried to bite him and had to be held down and sedated. The doctor gave the parents a vial of medicine to help the child but the medicine would only work for so long. Eventually, both parents knew what had to be done but only one of them accepted the idea. The other wanted desperately for there to be another way.

The mother had once gotten a holy man to come and pray for the house and their son but that did only raise her spirits. It did not and could not cure the child. On that day, the holy man had been afraid of the boy but he did not reveal this fear.

The father knew, after the episode with the cattle, what must happen, though he could not do it himself. He had told his wife the deal and laid it out fine but she would not accept it. That is, until one time, when she saw her son change before her, the drool, the snarling, the growth. At this time, she knew.

The week prior, they had prepared themselves and their son. The mother had made his favorite meal for him every day that week. And the father had taken him hunting and fishing and the son had been happy and seemed normal enough - but they both knew better. They had known the changing would happen, as it had, at night, when the moon rose full and all was quiet. At those times, he roamed. It was for this reason that they had kept themselves locked in their rooms, it would offer protection, just enough for him not to break in. But sometimes, they wondered, if the child truly wanted to harm them after changing, he could. They could not prevent him from doing so. Furthermore, no amount or strength of medicine could. The thought of this worried the father.

Presently their son rested, given sedation medicine an hour before, a bit too much, but purposely. His legs and arms were bound with leather straps (suggested by the holy man) but that would only hold for so long, so long as he stayed human. The mother had kissed his forehead and the father had done the same, both solemn. Both regretted what had to be done but only the father accepted this reality. The mother still, in some way, wanted there to be a chance.

The whole week she had prayed. And at this time she prayed and hoped that something could save him, from this changing, this curse. But her prayers were interrupted once she thought of what her husband had once said: "What if he gets into town? What if he kills an actual person? We won't be able to see him again, the townsfolk, they would hunt him down."

And then her tears did flow and she felt herself weak for not stopping them. And when her husband saw her crying he went to her and did wrap his arms around her and both parents wept.

And then, upon hearing this, the boy began to move in his bed, shifting and twisting, his bindings held tight but only tight enough. His mouth foamed, his limbs elongated, his teeth sharpened and his skin bristled.

Soon there would be a knock at the door. Following that, a man would enter, in hand a gleaming blade of silver. And whose side would time favor?

The Abominable Tommy Eccles

David Turnbull

There came a tap-tap-tapping on the coffin lid.

"Ten minutes, Mr Eccles."

In the clammy darkness of the silk lined casket, Tommy's eyes snapped wide. Breath rattled from him. He reached back and removed the pointed little finger bone jabbing at his side.

There came another tap on the lid.

"Can you hear me, Mr Eccles? You asked me to let you know when it was ten minutes before curtain call."

"I hear thee, lad," Tommy called back, cold hand pressing against the lid.

Rusted hinges creaked as the lid fell open. Tommy sat up, blinking against the overhead light. He heard the scurry of feet dashing across the floor, followed by the hurried slamming of the dressing room door. Tommy smirked. The lad had made a run for it as usual.

Tommy straightened his slightly wilting bow tie. After a momentary pause he clambered out of the coffin and sat down in front of the mirror. His face was grey and marbled with lightning forks of jagged blue vein. Eyes blank and rheumy. Lips ripening to an apple rot black.

The festering fingers on his fetid hands fumbled with his makeup kit. Slowly he applied foundation and rouge. Traced his eyebrows with black eyeliner. Touched up his eyelashes with mascara. Disguised the putrefaction of his lips with a dash of red greasepaint. Made it into a hideous smile.

Ghoulish, he thought, staring at the grinning reflection, *a ghoulish ghoul*. He reached for his pencil and pad, licked the lead with his green tinged tongue and jotted down the alliteration. Maybe there was a joke there - waiting to be extracted.

Tommy looked around the crumbling, plaster blown walls.

They were festooned in nostalgia. Brittle, age yellowed posters from the music hall heyday of his career, reviews at the Hippodrome and the Tivoli and the National Standard. One wall dedicated to their provincial cousins, the New Theatre Oxford, the Liverpool Empire, the Coliseum in Airdrie and many more. His name was almost always somewhere near the top of the bill.

On the dresser sat a faded photograph in a discoloured frame. It depicted a stern faced woman, dressed in Edwardian clothing. Mrs Eccles. Tommy sighed. She'd had no appreciation whatsoever of his talent. It seemed to him her main purpose in life had been to berate and belittle him, making *him* out to be the bad one whenever he dared to stand up to her.

"You might be feckless, Tommy Eccles," she'd wail, if he argued against her constant nagging. "But I swear, there's a monster lurking inside you."

Tommy smiled.

She could never have guessed the full horror of what was waiting to be unleashed from within. The dreadful lust that seized him in the gut soaked mud of the Somme. The horrendous and shameful appetites that had overwhelmed him as he wandered dazed and shell shocked amongst the bloated corpses. The ravenous fiend he had eventually become.

But she sure as hell found out.

One rainy night, after the end of the war, he'd turned up on the doorstep of the Blackpool B&B she'd had nagged him into buying for her. Oh the delight he'd experienced from the look of shock on her face when she'd saw him there. She'd been told that he was missing in action, presumed dead.

"I'm home for me dinner," he'd told her, pushing her forcefully into the hallway.

Once he'd gorged on her in an orgy of gleeful vengeance, he'd kept her foot for luck. He still had it, wrinkled and wizened to the bone, amongst gruesome jumble of trophies and souvenirs that had accumulated in his coffin.

He could scarcely believe it had almost been a hundred years since that night.

He'd stayed a few days at the B&B, devouring the guests one by one. For a while afterwards he'd skulked around dreary graveyards and prowled the grounds sanatoriums. Frequently dining at the morticians' slab. He was in no doubt that had the winds of fate not blown him toward the Theatre de la Nuit he would have been dead long ago. After all, monsters have a propensity for being hunted down and destroyed.

But now he was under the protection of Madame Morte.

The deal was a good 'un. He glanced up at the calendar that hung next to his mirror. The day's date was circled in red. Tonight was *wages* night. Tommy chuckled and rubbed his hands together. Over the past week he'd worked up a fair old appetite. From a drawer he produced a fusty but neatly folded cotton napkin. He set this down on the dresser and then laid his knife and fork at the ready.

A tapping on the dressing room door interrupted his preparations.

"On in two minutes, Mr Eccles," said the boy.

"I hear thee, lad."

***

Tommy pressed his battered bowler down over his ears and tilted it at a slightly ridiculous angle. After a quick dust of the frayed lapels of his suit, he headed out into the corridor. He could hear the wafting final refrain of a sultry torch song.

By the time he reached the wings Kathy Kelly, the Catford Contortionist, was bathed in yellow spotlight, naked as sin, limbs impossibly twisted into complicated erotic knots, a moulting feather boa serving as the thin line between artistic expression and gross indecency.

He heard a cheer go up as she unravelled herself and took her bow.

Sally B, the theatre's eternally youthful Mistress of Ceremonies, came on, resplendent in her tuxedo and cummerbund. Tommy prepared to make his entry, jumping a little when Kathy Kelly gave him a playful pinch on the bum as she bustled buxomly past.

From the stage Sally gave him a withering look. There was no love lost between the two of them but he knew she was a consummate professional. She wouldn't let their shared animosity get in the way. The microphone whistled feedback as she grabbed it from the stand.

Microphones. Tommy shook his head. *Never had microphones back in the day. A fella' had to learn to project his voice.*

"Now, folks, get ready to have your fancy well and truly tickled," announced Sally. "Here he is - the master of the bawdy rhyme, the Lancashire lad himself. Ladies and Gentlemen, the one and only, Tommy Eccles."

Cheers and clapping.

Sally turned to leave the stage, smiling smugly as if she was in on something he didn't know about. Tommy had no time to dwell on this. The band struck up the opening chords of his signature song. He entered stage right, one hand on his hat, pretended to trip on something, then looked out to the audience, feigning annoyance.

"Who put that there?"

He turned side stage and made as if he was calling to one of the stagehands.

"I said who put that there? I could have broken me ruddy neck."

A ripple of laughter emitted from those seated to the front of the stage. Not so much from those towards the back. Maybe the microphone wasn't such a bad idea after all. It whistled again as he

101

removed it from the stand. He held it up to his painted lips and launched into one of his legendary rhymes.

Mary found a severed limb
All mangled up and bloody
She'd have used it for something rather rude
If the fingers weren't so muddy!

Now the entire house erupted in vulgar laughter.

Tommy responded with his famous catch phrase.

"I always say that there's now't like a reet good laugh."

The audience cheered its familiarity.

One thing Tommy had learned over the years was that if the punters knew your material, you could keep them in the palm of your hand - so long as you gave them what they wanted. He nodded to the bandleader down in the pit. The band struck up his signature tune again.

Tommy launched himself with gusto into the self-penned lyrics, inspired in no small measure by events leading up to the purchase of the infamous Blackpool B&B and probably every other bloody thing Mrs Eccles had nagged him into spending his hard earned cash on.

The price was right and so we bought it
Then we went and found it cheaper somewhere else

I said to her the day we bought it
I bet we'll find it cheaper somewhere else
But the price was right and so we bought it

102

Then we found it bloody cheaper somewhere else

The parts of the audience that knew the song joined in with the last line.

"Story of my ruddy life," quipped Tommy bitterly, when the band had quietened.

Old wounds never healed.

A heckler called out.

"Tell us a joke, buddy, because you sure can't sing!"

The accent sounded American.

One of Madam Morte's special guests, no doubt.

It didn't do to let them get too uppity, even if they were on the VIP list. Tommy placed a festering hand on his hip and leaned forward, peering into the gloom. He clocked him, three rows back, dressed in a high-ranking military uniform. Next to him was an extremely tall and butch looking transvestite, face caked in badly applied make up, blond wig slightly off center.

"I know where you've been sticking your bloody bayonet," quipped Tommy. "I can see it in your eyes!"

aughter surged like a wave from front row to back.

The transvestite pretended to blush. The Yankee officer turned and scowled at her. Tommy knew he had to pick up the pace. He had to keep the gags coming thick and fast. He cocked his head as if he was listening to something. "Here," he said. "Can you hear all that bangin' and thumpin'?

Somebody's at it back stage wi' one of the dancers."

He turned around a called out. "Quieten down, pal. Make a bloke go deaf, so you could."

Pretending the audience couldn't hear him he stepped closer to the front row and yelled into the microphone at the top of his voice, free hand cupped to the side his lips.

"I said they could make a bloke go bloody deaf!"

Again laughter rippled from front to back. Tommy angled himself slightly to the right. He decided to pick up a military theme in honour of the heckler. Make sure he didn't get the notion to call out any more jibes.

"She were only a corporal's daughter," he said. "But she went down a ruddy storm in the officers' mess."

Laughter and a few hoots and wolf whistles followed.

With barely a skip in beat, Tommy threw them a limerick.

There was a young private from York
Who were peeing one night in the dark
He let out a yell
And cried what the hell?
When his mate stabbed his sausage wi' a fork.

A howl of hilarity went up when he recited the last line, mostly from the women.

"Here," said Tommy, "he didn't see that coming. I say - he didn't see that bloody coming."

More belly laughs echoed back at him from the crowd.

"You know what I always say?" asked Tommy.

"There's now't like a reet good laugh!" roared a section of the crowd.

"Knock, knock," went Tommy, keeping up the call and response theme.

"Who's there?" asked the crowd.

"Tsar," said Tommy.

"Tsar who?" asked the crowd.

Slurring his words Tommy weaved across the stage, affecting intoxication.

"Tsar's the last drink I'm 'avin'"

This time a cheer accompanied the laughter.

Tommy put his hand in his pocket and engaged the audience in a conversational tone, as if he were relaying a genuine anecdote.

"Who remembers the Great War?"

Silence.

"Well, I knew a fella' came back from the trenches wi' two wooden legs. A zeppelin flew over his street and dropped a big ruddy incendiary bomb. Poor bugger burned to the ground before his 'ouse did."

More laugher.

"That weren't the 'alf of it," Tommy went on. "He's sitting there on his bum amongst the ashes of his legs and a copper comes along and arrests the poor sod for *arson*."

There followed a brief lull in the laughter before the double meaning sank in.

Tommy used the pause to scan the theatre for his *wages*.

He found her near the back, seated with some of Madam Morte's regulars. Beneath the dull luminosity of the house lights the Madam's mark glowed greenly on the powdered flesh of her forehead. She was a redhead – voluptuous but not too top heavy. Tommy wondered what he'd done to please the Madam; usually his *wages* were either too stringy or laden with fat.

He smacked his lips and turned his attention back to the audience.

"Are there any ladies in the house tonight?"

He saw some of the men turn to their escorts.

No one, it seemed, dared raise a hand.

Then the transvestite rose somewhat unsteadily to her feet, sloshing about a glass of champagne. "Here I am, sweetie," she called, waving at Tommy and blowing him a dramatic kiss. Tommy grinned. Someone always took the bait. He affected a Scottish accent.

"I said ladies, no' *laddies*."

Another wave of laughter and another satisfying scowl from the yank.

Tommy cast a quick glance at his *wages*. She smiled demurely back at him. Madam Morte had clearly been to work on her. A promise of a place on the chorus line, followed by a bit of glam and mesmerising was all it took. She was his now and ripe for the plucking. After the show she'd be at the door of Tommy's dressing room, eager to please.

Tommy felt his tummy rumble. Curdled saliva sloshed about in his mouth.

"Get on with it!" yelled the yank.

Tommy shot a cheeky wink at the transvestite.

"I think we're all wondering just what it is you'll be getting on with after the show." The

106

laughter this time was a bit subdued. The audience were growing weary of the two-way point scoring. He couldn't afford to lose them now, so he launched into another of his naughty little rhymes.

Fe Fi Fo Fum
She's got a baby in her tum
Who put it in?
Little Johnny Green
Who hooked it out?
Old Mother Sprout

He placed his hand on his hip and brought the microphone up to his lip.

"Here," he said. "Can anyone tell me the difference between a seagull and a puppy?"

"They're both more entertaining than you," quipped the yank.

Tommy ignored him.

He held everyone for a few beats and gazed again at his *wages*. She gazed back and him and stroked a finger seductively down the furrow of her cleavage. Tommy began to drool. He imagined himself sinking his teeth into a plump pink breast and tearing away a bloody chunk of flesh.

A few impatient coughs from the front row snapped him back to attention.

"Got yer' flummoxed, have I?"

He paced the stage in one direction.

"The difference between a seagull and a puppy is..."

Another brief pause, then he turned and retraced his steps, head turned slightly to the audience. "...One flits across the shore and the other shits across the floor."

Howls of satisfying laughter assailed him.

He reattached the microphone to the stand.

"That were fun," he said. "I always say there's now't like a reet good laugh."

They cheered the catch phrase.

Right on cue the band struck up a reprise of his song. Before launching in to the words to bring his set to a close, he gave his *wages* a little knowing nod. Her smile smouldered as she nodded back. His tummy rumbled a little more.

Then he was off, singing into the microphone and waving his other arm back and forth for the audience to join in.

The price was right and so we bought it

Then we went and found it cheaper somewhere else

I said to her the day we bought it

I bet we'll find it cheaper somewhere else

But the price was right and so we bought it

Then we found it bloody cheaper somewhere else

Tommy took a bow, headed to the side of the stage, stopped in his tracks as if he'd forgotten something, and hurried back to the microphone.

"Here," he said. "It's a long ruddy way to Tipperary."

As they cheered him off he cast a quick glance backwards just in time to see his *wages* rising lithely from her seat.

***

108

Tommy rushed past the scantily clad dancers waiting to replace him on stage. He heard Sally making her introductions. Inside his dressing room he found himself pacing the floor.

He made his preparations. Unfolding his mildewed napkin. Placing the fork to one side and the knife to the other. Quickly he covered his coffin with a crumpled blanket. It wouldn't do for her to get the frights too early. *Wages* had been known to make a run for it in the past.

He had a terrible habit of blowing them in one go, wolfing down the lot, so that he was left with only the marrow to suck from the bones till the next pay day. He fancied he would savour this one, though, take her a little piece at time. Perhaps even take her in more ways than one. It had been a long time, but Tommy wasn't adverse to a little necrophilia every now and then.

When he saw the photo of his wife he angled it so that she would be facing the action. He liked to think that even the beyond the grave she could still be prudishly shocked by the wanton depravity he'd become capable of.

"Mr Eccles," called the boy's voice from out in the hall. "There's a lady admirer here to see you."

Tommy checked himself in the mirror. Removed his battered bowler. Patted down his stringy hair. Straightened his wilting bowtie. Gave himself a few squirts of cologne.

"Send her in," he called back.

The door swung inward. Tommy heard the slap of the boy's feet as he scampered down the hall. His *wages* stepped inside and pushed the door shut behind her, the Madam's mark still glowing on her forehead. When she tossed her red hair back over her shoulders he was a bit taken aback to see that she seemed considerably older than she had under the dim lights of the theatre. Despite this she still looked a damn sight more appetising than the gristly nags and sows he usually had to contend with.

"You look delicious," he said, openly appraising her.

Any notion that he might have moved too fast and used the wrong term was quickly dispelled when she returned the compliment.

"So do you."

He stepped closer and brushed her powdered cheek with the back of his fingers. She turned her head slightly and took his index finger between her teeth. At first he thought she was being playfully seductive. But then she sank in her teeth and bit right through to the bone. Tommy let out a yelp and snatched his hand back. Tart blood fizzed from the wound.

Shocked, he stumbled back against the covered coffin. She advanced on him. He saw how the flesh on her cheek, exposed when he'd rubbed away some of her make up, was as veined and marbled as his. She grinned and her teeth were black with rot. He looked into her eyes and saw that they swam with crimson bloodshot.

"Y-you're like me?" he stammered, hardly able to credit it was possible.

She licked his blood from her lips.

"I'm your replacement, Tommy. Madame Morte has decided to rescind your contract."

"Rescind my contract?" Tommy removed his bowtie and wrapped around his wounded finger. "She can't rescind my contact. It was signed in my blood."

She shook her head.

"You know as well as I do that Madam Morte can do as she pleases. Your contract isn't worth the flayed flesh it was written on."

Tommy swallowed down the lump that rose in his throat.

"But why?"

She sighed as if the answer was obvious.

"Your material is dated," she said. "This is the 21st century, Tommy. Nobody tells jokes about the Great War. Nobody even calls it the Great War any more. It happened a long time ago."

"Seems like only yesterday to me," said Tommy.

"That's as maybe," she said. "But nobody finds you material funny. It's not snappy enough. It's not edgy enough."

Tommy felt himself stiffen.

"They were laughing the ruddy house down tonight, that's for sure."

She sighed and shook her head again.

"They were laughing at *you*, not your material. Some of them out of pity, a few of them out of misplaced loyalty. You're yesterday's man, Tommy Eccles. Your head is in the past. Your jokes are from the ark. You're crude and offensive and more than a teeny bit sexist. You're a throwback. Why, I'll bet you've never once logged into the Internet."

Tommy grinned as a gag instantly formed in his head.

"Internet?" he shot back. "The only internet I'm interested in is the one that goes in t'net at Accrington Stanley on a Saturday afternoon."

She huffed and rolled her bloodshot eyes.

"My point exactly."

"So you think you've got better material than me?" challenged Tommy.

A smug expression washed over her face. As it did more of the powder fell away, revealing the rampant rot beneath. Her stench rose over her perfume. It filled the dressing room, as thickly as his own stink filled his coffin when he lay down at night.

"Before the *appetites* seized me I had an excellent reputation on the stand up circuit," she boasted. "I was on the panel on Mock the Week once. Miss B was suitably impressed when I auditioned for her. She gave a glowing report to Madam Morte."

"I've been around a hell of a lot longer that Miss bloody B," growled Tommy. "Before she came here the highlight of her career was singing songs in her knickers at some cheap cabaret club in Berlin."

His *wages* looked him up and down and sneer formed on her cracked and fissured lips. "Sally B is better dressed than you, that's for sure. Look at the state of your clothes."

Her nose creased in studied disgust.

112

"They've stood in me in good stead," said Tommy, brushing his tattered lapels. "What were you planning on wearing?"

"I was thinking of a scarlet basque," she replied. "With black stockings and suspenders. Finished off with some glossy red stilettos, heels as high as they go."

Tommy's hackles rose - Sally B sticking her damned oar in again. No wonder she'd looked so smug earlier on. "You can't do comedy dressed like that," he said.

"Of course I can," came the confident reply. "In case you hadn't noticed, this is a burlesque club. Half the acts dress like that. On a good night half the audience dress like that - men included."

"This isn't right," said Tommy. "I'm going t'see Madame Morte, right now."

He tried to barge past her, but she blocked his way.

"It would do you no good," she insisted. "Madam Morte sees no-one. In any case her mind is made up. The price might have been right when she bought you. But now she's found it cheaper somewhere else."

Tommy balled his fists. The audacity, turning his own words back on him. Why did women always do that? His wife, Sally bloody B, this one? His *wages* just stared him brazenly down.

"I'm a damn sight cheaper than you, Tommy," she said. "I only expect to be paid monthly, rather than weekly. One young man will do me. I like to hang them up by the ankles and leave them till they go a bit gamey."

113

Tommy's pent up anger flared. It was time to show this little upstart who was boss. His hand dipped swiftly into his jacket pocket and grabbed the knife that waited there.

He lunged at her.

But the blade of *his* knife was far shorter than the one on the knife which had suddenly appeared in *her* hand. He felt it penetrate his belly. She slashed up and then swiftly down, gutting him like a fish. His knees buckled and she swiped the blade across his neck, severing his windpipe.

Tommy dropped the floor, gargling pink froth, oily blood widening from puddle to pool on the floor. He saw her step over his twitching body. He heard the chink of his cutlery as she picked it up. She sat down on the coffin, gloating over him, diligently tucking his napkin into her cleavage.

"Here's a joke for you, Tommy," she said, sharpening the blade of the dinner knife against the side of the fork. "It's as old as the hills, but I think, in the circumstances, you'll appreciate the irony of the sentiments."

"Did you hear the one about the young lady who invited the old codger to dinner?"

"'What's on the menu?' he asked."

"'You are,' she replied."

Tommy could only gargle blood as he struggled to prevent the rotting yards of his ancient intestines from slopping out over the floor. She stabbed the prongs of the fork forcefully into his cheek, sliced through the flesh with the sharpened blade of the knife, and raised the portion to her lips. She chewed noisily down, then swallowed and started to laugh.

The laughter rose to a maniacal climax before she leaned in so close to his face that their ghoulish noses touched. "There's now't like a reet good laugh, Tommy," she taunted and stabbed the fork into his cheek once more.

Somewhere, Tommy fancied, Mrs Eccles was probably laughing, too.

Hiding Place

Rickey Rivers Jr

Years ago my brother was in hospital. I spent a few nights with him. One night, after he took his medicine, I left his room and went walking through the hospital. Night time was quiet and felt empty. I remember the sounds of TVs, beeping machines and nurses walking back and forth. It was pretty peaceful.

After walking for a while I found the snack and drink machines. They were on every other floor, starting with the lobby on up. I had to go up one floor to get to them. I made my choice of drink and stood there. The machine made a noise, but didn't give me anything. I tried the number code again, no drink. I tried a different code for a drink I didn't want, nothing. I pushed the coin return button, nothing. I was fed up and shook the machine as best I could.

I was careful not to cause too much noise, but still no drink. I gave up and kicked the machine. Then I looked around for cameras. I should have done that first. I didn't see anything, but my drink did drop. I heard the sound shortly after the kick. But that wasn't the only sound. Two things dropped: my drink and a biohazard bag. The bag wasn't fully sealed. The contents spilled and they were touching my drink.

After seeing that, I turned away from the machine and went back to the elevators. I remember holding my breath. I was dizzy when I reached the floor my brother was on. I was nauseous too. I settled for water from the water fountain but it didn't help.

None of the nurses stopped me on the walk back. I'm sure they had questions, but they left me alone. I think they knew something. I went back to my brother's room and let loose a loud sigh of relief.

My brother didn't wake up for a while. When he did I told him everything. He still doesn't believe me.

The rest of the night I thought about the biohazard bag. Why was it shoved into a drink machine? Who would put it there? Were they saving the contents for later? I didn't know. I didn't care. I just wanted my brother to hurry up and get better. I didn't want to spend another night there.

I didn't get much sleep.

If you're wondering, my brother's okay now. I haven't brought up the story to him again. I think he thought it was a dream anyway. You're the only other person who knows. You and whoever put the bag there. You don't have to believe me. I know what I saw. The image is fresh in my mind, fresher than what spilled out of the biohazard bag.

I still think about it, too. They were like skin colored carrots. And they weren't even a set. They were different sizes and skin tones. Like an assortment of chips, a multi-pack. Almost like a snack for someone. What else could it be? Someone was saving those fingers for something. Someone was hiding them in a spot without cameras. I remember indentations. Someone was chewing those fingers.

Bloodmoor

Olivia Arieti

The moorland, wild and poignant, was a disquieting scenery and all the wayfarers who ventured along its rugged and trackless paths feared to lose their way and their souls to the devilish creatures roaming upon the eerie heath.

Maureen lived in a small hamlet scattered among the many dales of the untamed land where the wind whistled mercilessly as if trying to awaken the dead and urge them to go back to their hearths, fields or valleys. When it ceased, though, a silence deeper than death fell upon the barren landscape and every single soul was scared even of its own shadow.

The area was so desolate that despair, horror and the rumours of the many gory deeds that had occurred, made it known as 'Bloodmoor'.

The girl, careless of spectres, demons and of all the creepy stories, used to take long walks there; the moor's wilderness somehow soothed her grief as she was devastated by the death of her previous fiancé and soon after, of her husband's one. Both lads had lost their lives on the battlefields.

On her last outing, the sight of an old log cabin surprised her.

No sooner she stood before it than the door flung open and she shuddered on seeing the two men; they were fighting.

"You told Maureen I died on the front after killing me so you could marry her," shouted Evan, "but I swore you wouldn't get away with it."

"Wait, I…"

Brad hadn't finished talking yet when a bullet pierced his heart - or what had remained of it.

Their uniforms were torn and tinged with blood and the bodies half decomposed with dangling limbs and bony sockets.

She was horrified and about to run away when Evan said, "Maureen, honey, don't be afraid, I loved you too much to let you waste your tears on such an asshole."

She cast a glance at the corpse on the floor and noticed that the blood around the wound had already coagulated…

Also the clots of blood of the cut on her fiancé's face were still visible…

She wondered what was going on. For sure, Evan wanted her to know what had happened…

"So Brad killed you…" she mumbled.

"Any other way to have you, baby?"

"Forgive me, darling, I felt so lonely… I guess I didn't know what I was doing."

"Kiss me one last time before I totally lose my body and you'll be forgiven on the spot." The tone was hollow despite the effort to make it as inviting as possible.

The girl gazed at him; the mouth was slightly dripping and the hair stuck upon his forehead as if glued. The handsome features were still visible but the hand of death had already started its work.

As Evan moved close to her, her heart began throbbing with love and disgust; she stepped back but the clammy hand was already caressing her face and immediately after his broken lips were on hers... An insalubrious warmth pervaded her as she shrank with horror.

Was she kissing a ghost, a zombie or was it all a horrid nightmare?

Maureen closed her eyes and felt her senses leaving her.

When she recovered, the room was empty. On the floor were the military jackets, the pistol beside them.

She stumbled out. Never had the landscape appeared more spectral. The sun had set and the heather carpet had turned purple like the dregs of wine or coagulated blood.

Sleepless nights followed and doubt tormented Maureen to the point that she had to return to the spot where the gruesome event had happened, but the cabin was no longer there...

Her heart leapt on discerning Evan staggering towards her like a wounded soldier returning to his beloved after a long and sanguinary war.

"I have come for you," he cried and stretched out his hand.

The couple were enfolded by a sudden fog and vanished in its sullen ghastliness.

Cigarette Run

Kevin L. Jones

The blistering sun sank behind the distant hills and mesas of the Arizona desert yet the temperature remained well over one hundred degrees in Bullhead City. Strong gusts of wind blew over Gene Burgess' body but the oven like air provided little relief from the heat. The dimly lit empty street that he often walked down seemed even more deserted and gloomy than usual. He had not seen a single car or pedestrian on the way to the gas station a short distance from the apartment he shared with his girlfriend Tara.

He ambled along at a leisurely pace, passing several vacant lots filled with scrub brush and sun baked earth. He muttered hateful things about his girlfriend that he did not really mean. Tara was the reason for this excursion. She had run out of Eagle 20s. Gene had offered to let her have some of his Camels but Tara had refused to smoke anything but her brand. She had more than broadly hinted that he would not get any loving tonight if he did not go down to the gas station and buy her some cigarettes.

Gene came around a bend in the road and noticed something that looked like a pile of rags. The moon came out from behind the clouds, bathing the street in pale silver light. Gene stopped dead in his tracks. It was not a clump of discarded clothing.

It was the torn and mangled corpse of an elderly woman in a twisted heap on the blacktop, a split open bag from the nearby Dollar store next to her body. The wind blew a can of Spaghetti Os down the gutter until it passed from under the street light's weak yellow glow and vanished into the darkness.

Gene tried to make himself believe that the old woman had been a victim of a hit and run but no car could have caused this amount of damage to her mutilated body. A soft mechanical purring sound began to echo down the lonely street. Gene's eyes grew wide as saucers as he saw a horrid sight that would haunt him for the rest of his days on earth. A red horned Devil rolled down the middle of the road in the deceased old woman's motorized wheelchair. Gene froze like a deer in the headlights. A few seconds earlier the world had seemed like a somewhat sane and safe place but if demons were real then anything could exist.

The unclean spirit slashed Gene's hand with one of its razor sharp claws as it sped past. The wheelchair's tires squealed as the demon skidded to a halt and began to race back towards him. Gene looked down at the blood steadily flowing from his wounds.

A series of hoarse screams burst out of his throat as he began to stumble towards the gas station. The demon sped towards him. It called out in a 'finger down a chalkboard' voice, "Gene, I've come to take you to Hell."

Gene started to run faster than he ever had in his entire life. His feet furiously pounded on the blacktop as he began to pull away from the loathsome creature. The lights of the gas station were visible in the distance. Just when Gene began to feel a glimmer of hope that he might make it to safety, the night winds started to howl like a chorus of damned souls. Every tumbleweed in Arizona seemed to be gathering in the road before him. In a matter of seconds an impenetrable rampart had formed. Gene turned as he heard the demon roll to a stop behind him. When the creature smiled Gene nearly pissed his pants.

The beast sniffed at the air for a second before it scowled and muttered, "You're not ripe. I can't take you yet. But believe me, you will be one day. When you are I'll come back for you and take you down into the abyss just like that old harlot splattered all over the road."

The wind's fury grew to an unprecedented level and a cloud of dust enveloped Gene. Then, as suddenly as it started, the storm was over. Gene finally managed to wipe the sand and grit from his eyes and looked around, no sign of the demon or its victim. The towering wall of tumbleweeds had returned to parts unknown. If it had not been for the overturned wheelchair he would have thought he had imagined the whole thing.

Right then and there Gene vowed to turn over a new leaf. In the years that followed the people that knew him best would often comment that it was remarkable how he had pulled his life together and shed all his many bad habits but sometimes, in the small hours of the evening, he would lie awake in bed, wishing that he had a cigarette. Whenever this feeling came over him Gene would look at the scars on the back of his hand and the urge to smoke would fade away as suddenly as the demon had on that long ago August night.

Here, Kitty, Kitty

Tom Leaf

It is Tuesday, mid-morning and Peter is standing in the middle of a basement bed-sitting room, quietly sipping lemonade from a jam jar.

No living creature, except Peter, has occupied this threadbare space for some time and yet the pernicious smell of cat excrement permeates the room like a brown mist.

Peter doesn't mind the smell. He is wearing his slippers. They are tartan and threadbare.

He is quietly thinking about room eleven. Peter was moved from room eleven, one and a half weeks ago. Room eleven had been secure. It had been a unit - which means one - so Peter hadn't needed to share with anyone else. A man whose name was called Simon was paid to look after Peter. It was what Simon called his job. Simon's hair was bald colour and Simon liked to whistle.

There hadn't been a window in room eleven, but there had been four pictures on the wall. Peter remembers that the pictures made him feel calm. Simon had told Peter that the pictures showed the four seasonings - or something like that - and that the four seasonings mean nature. Peter likes nature. Nature means fruit and leaves and animals.

Animals, like Bauble, the kitten.

Simon had found Bauble stuffed under Peter's bed.

After Simon found Bauble, things had changed for Peter. Simon had said that he couldn't look after Peter anymore. Not in room eleven, anyway.

Peter remembers the day that Simon had moved him from room eleven to the bed-sitting room. He remembers how the brown-faced boy with the wet forehead in room eight and the cross-eyed, thin girl from room ten had both shouted at him from across the corridor. The small, wrinkly girl next door in room nine had been crying and scratching at her face which seemed like a silly thing to do, Peter had thought.

The van that Simon had bundled Peter into that day had smelt of spit. That was the day that the quiet throb in Peter's forehead had been replaced by the fat headache.

The fat headache is now always there.

When Simon brought Peter to the bed-sitting room, they had both felt sad. Simon had sighed – twice - and he'd said that it would be safer for Peter in the bed-sitting room.

Peter was here on what Simon had called a 'mobility visit' and then Simon had said that Peter would be staying here for a little while.

Until everyone had forgotten about Bauble.

Now, as he thinks about Bauble, Peter makes his mouth into a smile shape. His right hand, nails bitten to the quick, drifts to the front of his blue corduroy trousers and pauses there, unconsciously lingering in fluttering expectation.

127

Bauble had been all wriggly. Peter remembers how he had held Bauble's face really tightly to stop him from being wriggly. He remembers squeezing and squeezing and squeezing.

Pop goes the Bauble.

Simon had found Bauble the kitten. But Simon would never find the others: Tinky, Pom-Pom and Crunch. Nor the puppy, Mike.

During the summer, Peter had carefully built up his collection. When he hadn't been asleep in room eleven - or very wide awake in the white room with Dr Barnes - Peter had spent his 'recreation periods' hiding quietly behind some green bushes, waiting for the time when a new friend would stray into the big garden. Peter was the one who had removed their collars and given them new names. He had been the one who had found them.

Finder's keepers, easy squeezers.

Peter hadn't collected them all at the same time, though. That would have been silly. Peter had taken his time. He had been patient.

Patient Peter.

***

It is Wednesday, early evening and Peter half-heartedly pushes a wet chicken egg and a grey pig chop around a small greasy pan. He is 'fending for himself' as Simon would say.

Peter has forgotten how to switch on the electric hob.

The bed-sitting room belongs to Simon and, even though Simon doesn't live here, he lives

128

nearby and has promised Peter that he will check in on him at least once a week.

In the meantime, Simon says Peter needs a Lilo. Or to lie low. Or to lie on a low Lilo. Peter struggles to remember exactly what Simon had said because of the fat headache.

Peter wipes the back of his mouth with a trembling hand and turns to his right. Or maybe, his left. He intends to dish up his cold, jellied meal onto a plate that he has found.

The plate is small and yellow. As he turns, Peter knocks a picture frame from the worktop onto the floor.

Clumsy Peter.

A blurry photograph of two glum faced kittens wearing Victorian bonnets now lies face up on the faded kitchen linoleum. The glass in the picture frame is broken. Peter looks at the kittens in the photograph. They are standing bravely to attention and each one is holding a parasol.

Peter looks at their dead, black eyes and their sad mouths, which have been stitched shut.

He lowers himself onto creaking knees, shakily reaching out a pale hand to pick up the broken frame. At the junction of the wall with the floor, he notices something odd. Something has sprouted from the flaking wall. Thin, finger length white hairs push outwards from a crack in the plaster. Peter touches them. They feel velvety.

Their appearance is peculiar and yet he does not pull back. He touches them again, more slowly this time.

Stroking them.

Peter's mouth is tightly pursed and his lonely blue eyes are crinkled in puzzlement.

Below the soft, white hairs the linoleum has worn away and there, upon the exposed floorboard a small knothole is revealed, fully encircled within a dark stain no larger than the outline of a hen's egg. Peter touches the stain with his finger tip. The stain is wet and the knothole is soft.

Peter leans forward and places his smooth face within kissing distance of the hairs and the stain. He can feel the faintest movement of air, a gossamer breeze slipping through the knothole.

A sprout of hair.

A soft, wet knothole.

A faint breeze, almost a breath.

He rises unsteadily to his feet and fumbles the broken picture frame back onto the worktop, his eyes fixed on the transformed corner of the room. He pauses, absently scratching at the electricity scar on the back of his skull. Pausing is something Peter likes to do.

After some time, he remembers where he is. Now he feels tired. Peter goes to bed, his cheap tea left to solidify in the pan. He sinks into a haunted, restless sleep.

Sleepy Peter.

***

It is Thursday, early morning and Peter, half awake, is lying face down in his own saliva. He is fully clothed, one of his slippers has fallen off and his bed linen, stained and stiff, lies crumpled at the foot of the bed. Through sleep encrusted eyes, Peter sees that the strange thing is still there.

The sprout of hair is noticeably thicker and it has grown so long that it bends to meet the bare board beneath.

The stain has spread, more than doubling in size. Its elongated, outermost tip now touches the lower edge of the adjacent scuffed skirting board as if licking it. Three feet above the skirting board, between the sprout and the stain, a nubby protrusion has appeared. It is as if the glistening tip of a wet, black crayon were being pushed forward into the room from behind.

Sprout, stain and tip. The oddity of the situation amuses Peter. A snickering whisper squeezes itself from between his thin, dry lips. (This is what Peter believes a person's laugh should sound like.)

He leans in once more towards the peculiar thing. The slight breeze emanating from the soft, wet knothole has noticeably increased, for the hair sprout above is slowly swaying back and forth like pond weed under the surface of some dim, forgotten lake.

The surface of the knothole is mottled with dark dots, reminiscent of bread mould and the buttony nub protruding from the wall has a dull sheen to it like the dimming eye of a dying calf.

Tentatively, Peter lifts a trembling finger and places it gently upon the buttony nub. The nub flinches and a faint, plaintive mewling seeps from the mottled, wet lips of the knothole. Peter presses again, firmer this time. At this intrusion, the sprout becomes agitated, its diaphanous wisps snapping back and forth, insistently kittenish.

'It's alive,' whispers Peter to no-one else in the room.

As if in recognition of this epiphany, the knothole closes creakily in upon itself. There is a slight pause before the knothole swiftly snaps back open, vomiting forth a thickly slick trickle of black, spotted mess. Peter flinches, yelping in primal fear, repulsed by the spawn-like froth bubbling in wet abundance out of the timber throat.

Peter's gorge rises in reaction to the fetid stench of vomit and excrement wafting up from the rapidly growing pool of soft, glutinous muck in front of him. He pushes back, twisting away in horror, his single Velcro-strapped slipper floundering on the kitchen linoleum in an attempt to gain purchase. He scrabbles to his feet and, with barely a backward glance, he rushes, terrified, to the presumed refuge of the bathroom.

***

It is Thursday, mid-morning and for the last hour Peter has been in hiding, wedged between the toilet bowl and the curved edge of the cast iron bathtub.

His panicked, ragged breathing is doing little to mask the insistent sounds of activity from the bed-sitting room and the feeble daylight creeping under the bathroom door is increasingly punctuated by flickering shadows of feverish movement. Flapping slaps can be heard, as though something wet and heavy were lifting itself up, only to flop back down onto the kitchen linoleum.

The bathroom door has no keyhole and the gap beneath provides no adequate line of sight. Peter musters all his courage, creeps out from his hiding place and carefully places his ear against the door. The bed-sitting room is being systematically torn apart, as though whatever now inhabits the room is searching for something.

Or someone.

A pan lid clatters to the floor, spinning in ever decreasing circles, a cupboard door is dashed into splinters and the harsh metallic screech of a tap being torn adrift is followed by the splashing gush of water cannoning off the peeling, yellowed ceiling.

Peter's bare foot is wet. His refuge has been breached. A fast flowing stream of water is running under the gap in the door, flotsam – timber splinters, rotting food waste and torn chunks of the foul-smelling black spawn – washes across the bathroom floor, swilling up against the skirting boards and circling around the clawed feet of the bathtub.

The bathroom door hammers rapidly against Peter's face, a frenzied demand for entry from whatever horrific entity is running amok in the bed-sitting room. Startled, Peter backs away, eyes wide in shock. The hammering persists and the thin plywood door shakes violently, threatening to break free from its hinges. He whimpers uncontrollably and turns to stare at the cast iron bathtub, stained and sturdy. He wades towards it on trembling legs and climbs in, curling himself up as small as he can, trapped and petrified.

As abruptly as it had begun, the hammering on the door ceases. Peter's eyes are squeezed tightly shut. He remains perfectly still, silently counting off the passing seconds. From the bed-sitting room, the roar of cascading water continues unabated. Peter counts slowly up to seventy three – the largest number he knows – and then peeps over the roll top edge of the bathtub. He climbs out, knowing that he cannot spend the rest of his life in the bathroom. He pulls open the bathroom door, immediately regretting his decision.

***

The black spawn reigns supreme, completely covering the floor in spectacular fashion, its stinking, globular mass stretched thickly to every corner, bobbing serenely on the ever rising tide of gushing tap water.

In the corner of the room, the hair sprout rises in thick abundance from beneath the carpet of black spawn. It clings to the remains of the kitchenette in matted profusion and has scaled the wall towards the ceiling where it hangs, forming a gently swaying canopy.

The glistening, buttony nub protrudes egg-like from the wall. It intently scans the room, its darting gaze sporadic and fretful. The nub spots Peter and freezes. As if on cue, a flurry of sliding movement signals the entry of something new and Peter's wildly rolling eye spots twisting motion in the darkest corner of the room.

His linen has become insistent.

The soiled bed sheets have twisted themselves, snakelike, into a rope, four fingers thick, a cotton anaconda, terrifying in its eyeless determination. It raises its knotted back into shivering humps before flopping downwards into sidewinder ridges, it slithers swiftly across the surface of the black spawn pond to where Peter is cowering in the bathroom doorway.

He drops to his knees, covers his eyes and prays that the end, when it comes, will be swift and painless.

***

It is Thursday, early evening, and Simon - a bag of groceries clutched in his left hand – attempts to let himself into the basement flat. The front door is jammed and, despite his efforts to shoulder it open, Simon is unable to gain entry. The steady stream of water running underneath the door is concerning. Simon makes his way to the rear of the building and, using a tin of baked beans from the grocery bag, he shatters the bathroom window. The stench that wafts out to greet him is unbearable. Mindful of the shards of glass still jutting out from the frame, Simon pulls himself through the open window.

The bathroom is in darkness and there is no light seeping under the closed door leading to the bed-sitting room. Simon can hear the rush of water and can only assume that the electricity is off as a result. He fumbles for his mobile phone, just about seeing the faint outline of the bathtub in front of him. He unlocks his phone, turns on its torch and discovers what has become of Peter's body.

Peter's body is face down in the bathtub. His head, however, has been turned to face the ceiling, the neck a twisted, candy stick spiral of skin. His t-shirt has been pulled up behind his ears, tying his skull to the taps.

Peter's pale blue eyes, marbled with blood, have been squeezed from their sockets and are playfully lolling upon the dead cheeks below. His mouth has been forced open in an endless scream, throat stuffed to the brim with a thick clot of blood and hair. Peter's swollen torso, face up, stomach down, is slowly undulating from within, the skin tightly stretched outwards like a wet balloon.

This rippling, liquid undulation is causing Peter's body to lift and then drop back down. As it does, his belt buckle clinks against the bottom of the bath. Up. Then down. Slowly and repetitively. Clink, clink, clink in a bizarre parody of coitus.

It appeared something has taken root inside Peter and is keen to escape.

Simon stands transfixed in disgust, the bag of groceries forgotten, a clenched fist thrust firmly into his mouth in an attempt to stifle a scream. Each time Peter's body rises out of the bathtub, the spine is pressed almost to breaking point against the skin of his back.

The rising and falling of Peter's torso is becoming frantic. Faster and faster, up and down, up and down. Tiny spots of blood bloom into life across Peter's flesh as if pins were being pushed through from beneath, their number increasing in multitude, a constellation of blood dots peppering his bloated flesh.

Faster and faster, up and down, up and down, the belt buckle fervently tapping out a fevered metronomic beat upon the bottom of the bath. Faster and faster. Peter's tethered face jiggles on the limit of its twisted neck in a horrific parody of a carnival mask, the eyes comically swinging to and fro like pendulous eggs.

The pinpricks have now become so numerous that they entirely cover the surface of the back. Peter's skin is starting to split, the cadaver being forced open like a wet paper bag by the sheer strength of whatever horrific thing is hatching out. The bath is rapidly filling with Peter's blood, the hot, metallic reek of it flooding Simon's nostrils, his gorge rising, the sheer horror of the unfolding situation before him almost impossible to comprehend.

Faster and faster, up and down, up and down.

Clink, clink, clink.

Faster and faster, up and down, up and down.

Clink, clink, clink.

Simon screams, his sanity broken, as the slaughtered grey thing that once was Peter, now stretched beyond all reason, triumphantly bursts open like a hot, wet fruit.

The wonderful surprise is vomited forth, pushed up and against the fatty confines of the rib cage, every haunted element wondrous in its peculiarity. Five things. Empty eyed, gloriously dead, foetal. Four baby cat shapes. And a baby dog shape. Peter's friends are inside him. Where they always belonged. Welcome back, friends.

And, finally, rest.

In pieces.

Dead Peter.

***

The picture frame remains in place on the kitchen worktop. The kittens still stand to attention. They still resolutely clutch their parasols. Their eyes still glisten blackly like cold, dead stars. Now, however, their tiny grinning mouths, finally unstitched, reveal themselves to be full of small, sharp teeth.

The Child Snatchers

Rie Sheridan Rose

"Twelve degrees starboard, Larakin," ordered Captain Stilskin. "There's a hovel on the hill, looks promising."

"Aye, aye, Cap'n." The mate turned a brass crank and the complex system of gears powering the steerage of the island meshed to start the whole of it into a ponderous turn.

Stilskin stepped to the edge of the island, looking out over the sea of clouds that billowed around them. The sun was beginning its dying arc and the clouds were gold and bronze.

This was his favorite time to pounce, at the dying of the day when distances got hazy and children grew careless trying to squeeze out one more round of tag or one more game of hide and seek.

The bright sound of laughter rose through the air to the island from the hovel on the hill. Yes! A pack of laughing children spilled out of the shack and danced down the sides.

A pretty little red-haired girl in a torn smock caught the captain's eye.

"That one, Larakin. I'll have that one."

"Aye, sir."

The goblin strapped on his steam apparatus and jumped off the side. The whirligig attached to the top of the device began to spin and he manoeuvred until he was right over the girl's head. With a swooping dive, he snatched her up and was back into the clouds again before she had time to scream.

"Excellent work, Larakin!" the captain cried. "Put her with the others for now."

Larakin nodded and shoved the struggling child before him until they reached the crumbling ruin that was the island's only structure. He took a huge brass key from his shirt and unlocked the door to the cellar.

"In you go, dearie," he ordered, giving the girl a push.

That made a dozen in the cell. The goblin horde would eat well this month.

"Let's go home, Larakin," called the captain.

"Aye, aye, sir."

With another ponderous turn, the island headed for its mooring. The hunt was done for now.

The Albatross

Harry Steven Lazerus

"You better be careful," he warned. "I have magic powers. I can turn myself into a tiny wasp and fly up your nose. I'll eat your insides out."

We laughed, knew it was just Tiny Tim's attempt to stop the bullying.

"Up all our noses at the same time?" we jibed. "That's some magic power!"

But we'd stop, knowing we had gone too far. None of us really wanted to hurt Tiny Tim, except maybe first mate Jones McBride, who had complained to the captain and even the owners when Tiny Tim was added to the crew of the *Marie Manning*.

His real name was Timothy Scott. He was short and puny. Though able to do most of the work, he often became seasick, long before the rest of us did. No one understood why Tiny Tim had decided to sign on and, even more, why the ship's owners had accepted him. According to Jones, the owners refused to discuss it.

"There's some black reason behind it," Jones muttered, spitting out a gob of dark tobacco juice onto an already grimy deck.

***

A strong gale caught us off Cape Horn, on our way from from China. Our sturdy clipper tossed and turned like a child's boat in the bathtub of an energetic boy trying to propel the water over the side. Tiny Tim got violently sick. I felt sorry for the guy, so I added his tasks to mine.

Jones saw me doing Tiny Tim's work.

"You don't have enough to do already?" he growled at me.

I shrugged.

"The poor guy's sick."

Jones growled at me again but I paid it no mind. He respected me as a seaman, even told me once that if he ever became captain he wanted me as first mate.

I still hated his guts.

Jones stamped his feet and glared at the sea.

"I've had it with Tiny Tim," he spat. "I'm going to teach him a lesson he'll never forget."

The menace in his voice was more frightening than the raging sea and sky.

***

The sea calmed. Tiny Tim was still recovering in his bunk. Jones gathered the rest of the crew around him. Only the captain, in the forecastle, was missing.

Jones' eyes scanned the crew, stopping at mine.

"I'm going to teach that layabout a lesson he's never going to forget. Next port-of-call he's going to get off this ship and never, ever get back on."

I listened with disgust to Jones' plan.

***

The crew, minus the captain, gathered around the helpless, blindfolded figure of Tiny Tim. His hands were tied behind his back. He was shaking and crying.

"You'll regret this!" he called out weakly, unconvincingly. "The sea gives me power," he sobbed.

Many in the crew guffawed. I felt powerless to stop the travesty that had already begun.

"You're a burden to this crew, Tiny Tim," Jones snarled. "You shirk work, pretend to be sick, but eat our food. You take the place of an able-bodied seaman."

Jones paused and winked at the crew.

There was laughter.

I did not laugh. I do not see amusement in a mock execution.

"You're going to walk the plank, walk the plank into the sea. That will be your new home."

"No!" Tiny Tim cried.

I shivered at this strange contest between two such opposite men.

A long wooden plank led up to and over the edge of the ship. The very end of the plank hovered over the sea. Two seamen stood at each side near the plank's end.

The plan was for them to grab Tiny Tim when he reached the end, lift him up as if they were going to hurl him into the sea and, at the last moment, haul him back to the deck of the ship.

Jones took Tiny Tim by the elbow and led him along the plank. When he almost reached the end he resisted Jones' tug.

"There's no going back now!" Jones admonished.

"No," Tiny Tim cried. "There isn't." There was no fear in his voice now.

The two seamen lifted Tiny Tim and held him over the sea. A sonorous whine emitted from Tiny Tim's open mouth. It grew louder and louder, breaking into an ear-splitting shriek.

The seamen who had been holding Tiny Tim gasped in terror; their hands suddenly empty. In the air between hovered a tiny wasp, buzzing angrily.

It flew straight toward Jones McBride and disappeared into his left nostril.

Jones screamed, doubled up and fell to the deck, writhing in agony.

"Get it out!" he cried. "Get it out of me!"

He gasped, clutching at his throat.

The crew watched, dumbstruck. No one knew what to do. The captain, normally imperturbable and emotionless, watched with undisguised terror on his face.

The metamorphosized Tiny Tim travelled through Jones' body; we could chart its course by the jerky motions of Jones' arms and hands, now clutching his stomach, now his throat, now his groin...

I prayed that Jones' end would come swiftly, mercifully.

It did not.

A fresh gale came up and buffeted the ship. The wind howled. Jones' screams of agony grew louder than the wind. We all covered our ears but could not take our eyes away from the figure wriggling on the deck.

The agony seemed to go on forever.

"Throw it overboard!" the captain shouted at last. Three men, the muscles on their arms bulging, strained to lift the still alive Jones and toss him against the wind and rain into the sea.

Once the body hit the water the storm stopped. So did the screams. A few moments later a wasp flew over the side of the ship, over the deck and landed on me.

It did not sting. Instead, it gently brushed the skin of my neck with its wings.

Such a Gripping Read

S J Townend

Have you ever been so lost in a book that the protagonist is wearing your shoes and you theirs and you're sharing the journey together? Have you ever been so distracted that you bite your nails down to stumps as you delve six foot deep into that thriller? So trapped, that your coffee blows cold, untouched? So engaged, that your lonely heart cries like a wolf under a strong moon as you tear through the last few pages of that romance; that you catch sight of fantastical creatures with pointed ears which have leapt from the pages and is dancing in between the blades of grass as you leaf through that glorious, all-absorbing tale whilst sat on the bench at the park? Have you ever fallen so deeply into a book?

Have you ever been so mislaid in and taken onboard by a book that you know as soon as you have finished it, if not a little before, that you will scour the library, the local bookstore, the internet, to purchase and gather every single story, novella, essay and poetry collection that the author has ever written? You want to hang onto the author's every word like a coat on a hook, like a child's tightly curled fingers around the string of their brand new red balloon. You want to be able to savour the author's use of language, their expression of self, their poignant paragraph structure and distinct turn of phrase for just a little longer after the novel in your hand is done; you're so very lost in the universe it has created with its zoetrope of colour soaring upward from the black on white prose.

Have you ever rushed the preparation of food for your children and partner, bought and micro-waved a ready meal and passed it off as home cooking—no-one will most likely even notice—just so that you can sit down and read for a little bit longer and spend a little less time stood at the worktop, peeling, chopping, frying and stirring; so you can indulge a little longer, run your eyes over the words in that book for just a little longer, delve a little further into that storyline, be whisked away for just ten minutes more to discover what happens next?

Have you ever cancelled plans with friends a quarter of an hour prior to the agreed meeting time on a Friday evening to watch the band everyone's talking about as the sofa and your current novel are pulling you towards them with a force stronger than gravity, stronger than a body weighted with bricks to aid its journey to the depths of the ocean, with an unquantifiable force which is practically pleading with you to take that quiet night in with a book and a plate of carpaccio and pastrami slices instead of going out?

Have you ever been so engrossed in a story, so very tied up in the characters and the storyline and the ambience and the throws of it all that when your four-year-old daughter whom you bore from your very own womb, asks if she can use the toilets at the

147

park, you nod concordantly without even looking up from the novel in your hands and so, off she skips. Have you ever been so ensnared in a plot and that *quirky protagonist*, that unreliable narrator and that story arc that you have never explored before that you let your daughter enter the lightless block of cubicles behind the bushes, just out of sight, completely alone, in order to empty her bladder?

Have you ever been so distracted by an author's words that they whip you up, up and away from the greyness of the October skies that are holding onto a heavy shower for just a moment longer which are spread above you to let the story take you to an entirely different place, far from where you are sat? Have you ever been so tucked up in the relationship between the characters and so engaged with the two or three subplots the author has carefully crafted into that bound set of pages that rests on your lap as you sit on the bench that you don't think twice as your child skips off solo towards the unstaffed park facilities, the toilets with the flooded floors and empty soap dispensers, the smashed strip light and the ever-dripping tap?

Well, my dear—that is when you will find me, the antagonist in the grim tale that is your mundane storybook life. That is when your child will find me too, lurking in the beetle-black end cubicle, with my claws that silence instantly and my dead eyes that flush away dreams and souls. That is when your child will find me waiting for them. I have been waiting for all of time, for end times, to end their time.

148

My dear, will you put your book down after five minutes? Ten? After the red balloon has glided, floated up into the grey skies which swallow it whole, long before you stop to think about what you have done?

What I have done?

Oh, what have I done?

How long will it be, as you read page after page, chapter after chapter, until you realise your daughter has not returned?

A Stoning

R.G. Evans

Semray knew the other fifth-graders had found out about her mother the day they pelted her with kickballs during recess. Someone--Jacob Cook, probably--must have spied during library time while she was at the computer reading one of the articles about her mother she was forbidden to read at home:

"Saudi Woman Accused of Witchcraft, Stoned to Death"

"Stone the witch!" one of them cried, pegging her with a kickball on the side of the head. Stunned, Semray sat down hard as a group of boys took up the chant.

"Stone the witch! Stone the witch!"

They circled Semray, most still strangers to her. She and Jiddah Nuray had fled to the U.S. a month before and she'd attended Olivet school for only two weeks. The children chanted as Semray made herself small, the balls stinging wherever they hit.

"That's not how you stone a witch."

This voice she knew. Jacob Cook who tormented her every day, mocking her name, her hijab. *Rag head*, he'd sneer.

"*This* is how you stone a witch."

She saw Jacob's hate-filled eyes, his lips pulled back in a snarl. Over his shoulder, she saw Ms.

Purdy, their teacher, running toward them. Semray had time to think *She's too late*.

Then she saw the rock in Jacob's hand. It was only about the size of a golf ball, but Jacob threw it with such ferocity that when it smashed into her lower lip, it felt like a cannonball. Pain flared along Semray's jaw and her mouth filled with the coppery taste of blood.

"Jacob Cook!"

Through tears, Semray saw Ms. Purdy seize Jacob by the back of his long, pumpkin-orange hair so hard some of it came away in her hand.

"Principal's office--now!" She shoved Jacob to get him moving. Jacob sucked his teeth and looked daggers at Semray, but he reluctantly started walking back toward the school.

"Are you all right?" Ms. Purdy knelt beside Semray, cupping her chin with one hand to check the damage. Semray winced.

"They think I'm a witch," Semray started to sob.

"They're stupid little children," Ms. Purdy said. "Now let's get you to the nurse."

***

Later that day, Semray sat in the principal's office along with Ms. Purdy and Semray's grandmother, Jiddah Nuray, whose expression looked to be somewhere between anguish and rage.

"Mrs. Onal," the principal said, "let me say I am deeply troubled by what happened to"--she glanced at the folder on her desk--"to Semray. I

151

assure you the students who did this have been punished."

"But who was watching the children?" Jiddah Nuray said.

"I was on the playground," Ms. Purdy said. "I saw what happened."

Before her grandmother could turn her fury on Ms. Purdy, Semray said, "Ms. Purdy saved me, Jiddah."

"I assure you, Mrs. Onal," Ms. Purdy said, smiling at Semray and making her blush, "Semray will be protected."

***

On the day Jacob Cook returned from suspension, Ms. Purdy kept Semray in from recess. Semray liked Ms. Purdy. She was young and smartly dressed and Semray hoped Ms. Purdy liked her too.

"Semray, the children see you as different; what children don't understand, sometimes they fear."

Semray blinked.

"I know you are no witch, Semray," she said and leaned closer. "I know your mother wasn't either."

Semray's eyes filled with tears.

"Like children, men fear what they don't understand. They must have feared your mother, but not for being a witch."

Semray felt a tear roll down her cheek.

"Now," Ms. Purdy clapped her hands, smiling warmly. "I have a surprise for you!"

***

Before recess ended, Jacob Cook entered the classroom and went straight to Semray's desk.

"I was looking for you outside, rag head," he said so only Semray could hear.

"Jacob," Ms. Purdy said. "Take your seat, please."

Jacob glanced at the teacher then turned back to Semray.

"Where were you. Rag. *Head*?"

With the last word, Jacob snatched the hijab off Semray's head. She screamed and backed away from him, dark hair spilling down over her shoulders.

"Jacob!"

This time, Semray noticed, Ms. Purdy got Jacob's attention. She saw his head snap towards her and Semray followed his gaze to where Ms. Purdy stood at her desk. She was pointing a trembling finger at the orange-haired boy, her mouth shaping silent words.

Jacob coughed. One dry cough, then another. His eyes widened and his hand went to cover his mouth. When he coughed a third time, he held out his hand.

In his palm lay a tiny, smooth, white pebble.

Semray backed away as Jacob began to cough more violently.

153

A spray of slightly larger stones clattered to the floor.

Semray glanced at Ms. Purdy and saw she was no longer pointing at Jacob, but her lips were moving even more furiously.

When a golf ball sized stone fell out of Jacob's mouth and bounced under a desk, Semray thought of the surprise Ms. Purdy had shown her toward the end of recess. She'd pulled open one of her teacher's desk drawers and there, looking up at Semray, was a small, crudely fashioned doll, its face a cartoonish angry scowl. On top of its head a few wispy orange hairs moved in the air. Wedged into a gash in the doll's belly was the stone Jacob had thrown at her earlier that week.

Boys--and men, Ms. Purdy told her, *fear what they don't understand. People who don't look like them. People with different customs.*

Semray looked at Jacob just as he fell to his knees, a grapefruit-sized rock forcing its way out past his teeth. Semray heard them breaking.

They seldom fear those they think are like them, Ms Purdy had said. *The best way to hide is in plain sight.*

Jacob gagged and moaned on the floor beside her desk. Semray saw Ms. Purdy's lips were still moving, but now she seemed to be smiling at Semray.

When Ms. Purdy winked at her, Semray smiled back.

Loud Reality

Rickey Rivers Jr.

1.

[Carl W - Parent]
I got the news at work, worst day of my life. You don't plan for something like that. It was just a regular work day. Then you get news that shakes everything up.

***

[Florence V - Teacher]
We do fire and tornado drills. We never trained for something like this. Something so random, you can't train children for it. It's an inside threat, one of our own...

***

[Jasmine H – Student]
We were in math class. Our teacher told us to hide under our desks. I watched Mr. Watson lock the classroom door and turn off the lights. Then he hid under his desk too. Everyone was quiet and someone was crying close to me. I kept my eyes on the door. We heard shots outside the room. It sounded like they were all around us.

***

[Rachel R – Parent]

It's a horrible thing and I feel terrible for the children. I can't help but think it could have been prevented. People have to start asking questions beforehand. Was he bullied? Did he have any friends? What was his home life like? People need to be aware before something like this happens again. Next time it could be my child or yours.

***

[Clarence M – School District Representative]

Let it be known that this level of brutality does not reflect our school district. I'm sorry, I can't say more at this time. Thank you for your concern.

***

[Jackson E – Custodian]

There was a hallway echo. It got you disorientated. I had walked them halls a thousand times. This time it was different. All I could do was lie down in the custodial closet. I was in there with the cleaning supplies just shaking. The smell was so strong. That's still in my nose. Just a strong smell of stuff I been around for as long as I been cleaning. Everything outside was so loud, just loud and wrong.

***

[Tracy N – Parent]

Jail or hell I don't care which. Maybe his parents were good, I don't know. I don't care. I lost my child. He should pay for that. So many children have lost their lives and for no reason. I don't feel anything anymore. I'm angry.

2

[Name withheld – Former student]

Wow, that was so long ago, of course I remember. It was scary, you know, to be in the thick of it. A friend of mine died, she was shot through the chest. It was terrible.

I didn't know the shooter. I knew that he went to the same school, but I never spoke to him. I heard he was just as normal as us, whatever that means. Folks like to say "he didn't seem like the type" but what's 'the type' you know? My eyes aren't what they used to be, but even back then I didn't recognize 'the type'. I wish those who knew what the 'type' was would have said something back then. That sounds cruel, forgive me. Thinking about it just makes me upset.

After something like that happens everyone always has an opinion. Beforehand, though, nobody has anything to say. They're just clueless, living their lives. Folks don't think to care until after. Like people who show up to funerals who haven't spoken to family in years. Like, did you really care? Or did you wait for them to die, so you could pretend to?

At the time I hid behind the bleachers in the gym. I'm surprised he didn't look back there or at least shoot back there. I saw the other students running. Everybody scattered like ants. Bullets flew at random. I guess he didn't have a plan.

I remember thinking I was dead, like I was viewing everything from the afterlife. It was like an out of body experience. It felt weird to watch. I couldn't save anybody. I was too busy looking. Kids were breathing one second and dead the next.

Three weeks after that school let back in. Everything was scrubbed clean and disinfected. The walls and floors had memories washed away.

I lied to my parents about everything. I told them I didn't see anything. I told them I just heard the shots. It doesn't matter now. The truth wouldn't stop anything. And I know I wasn't the only one hiding. There were others. There were teachers and students hiding. I don't blame them. No one can take blame, no one could do anything. You either sat and watched or ran and got shot. Those were the options. And pray, yeah, you had plenty of time to pray.

It's strange, now that I'm remembering. None of it really seems far away. It feels recent. These things feel so normal. Then again, maybe it's just memories coming back. No extent of support group can fully wipe your mind; fully clean the blood out of your head.

The walls and floors of the school are still stained beneath the bleach. Visions of the past, long forgotten, that's the lie we choose to believe. I lay in bed at night, still hearing the echo, the screaming, the shoes squeaking and the quiet of no children.

I can never go back to that school. Spirits lurk the halls. I believe this, truly. I mean that's what you do. You stay in school if you don't graduate. And isn't that a terrible thing? To be trapped in school with no way out? You want to leave but you can't. You want someone to just pick you up. You want the nightmare to end.

Then you realize the nightmare is instead a waking reality and you find a place to hide. What else can you do? Surely, it'll be over soon. Surely, the gunshots will stop. Surely, you'll get to go home again. You'll make it to graduation. The mind reassures. We lie to ourselves all over again. The survivors have to deal with this reality, this loud reality that echoes down the halls.

The Way of Things

Michael H Hanson

"Predator and prey move in silent gestures, on the seductive dance of death, in the shadows cast by the vultures of the night." –*Luis Marques*

Danu AosSi, eldest of her kind and certainly the most beautiful, races across early morning fields of dew-tipped down and willow grass. Her azure form is lithe and her nimble feet barely leave a sign of her passage. If any mortal had witnessed her passing, they would only see a bluish blur, as if a tiny storm cloud had dropped from the skies to fly over the ground. In moments, just before the first cock crows, she reaches the boundaries of the mother forest covering over half of the Emerald Isle.

A close call, she thinks, striding confidently through thick brush and around towering oak trees that mark the leading edge of the forest and which protect her kind from the damning firelight of day.

Many a Walsh lay dead upon a field of battle, surprised by a late night bushwhack of bloodthirsty Kellys. The slaughter was as quick as it was devastating. And Danu traveled to farm and homestead to wail the passing of mortal souls in her guise of Mórrígan, a ragged old hag in a dark hooded cloak.

But then comes the hint of dawn as she finishes her final rounds and she is free to shrug off the disgusting avatar of death and retire to the vastness of the forest, the true heart and home of fairyland.

Danu ponders for a moment on the flood of mortals that poured into Eire ten thousand years ago. It was a once magical land isolated and protected by the ocean for many millennia, but the intrusion of people slowly, over hundreds of years, forced her kind underground, or behind magical barriers that separated the real world from small, cleverly disguised alternate dimensions. But the greatest wonder of all was humanity's pull upon the essence of the AosSi, for such was men and women's souls glowing beacons of divinity, that mystical bonds were created between immortal faerie kind and mortal folk and so those like Danu became twined with human ritual and rite.

She sighs. Such a journey-filled night is not without its toll and so Danu crouches near a sparkling stream and sings a song of innocent laughter and childlike seduction.

In moments a tiny purple figure, no taller than a hand-span, appears before her. It is shaped like a naked man, but hairless, the four-winged form of a *Nixie*, the smallest of the AosSi.

Danu smiles and, without warning, her delicate azure hand snaps forward to entrap the shocked sprite, which squeaks in terror. Its shiny small eyes open wide as it struggles to break free. It then bites down on one of Danu's fingers, drawing green blood, but the pain bothers her not.

"Little one," Danu coos as her grin grows broader and displays two rows of razor-sharp black teeth, "it is the way of things."

She bends forward, bites off the tiny bald purple head in mid-squeal and spits it into the stream. She presses her lips greedily to the frothing neck of the spasming headless figure and sucks out every drop of the sweet amber liquid manna which runs through its veins and arteries. A few moments later she is done.

Danu tosses the decapitated desiccated fairy corpse into the stream and licks her lips one final time. There is nothing like a good meal after a tough day on the job. The rising sun bleeds over the distant horizon and Danu resumes her flight.

Faerie, Men, Salamanders, Danu thinks as she strides deep into the forest and into the endless welcome darkness between eldritch canopy, *perhaps we are not all that different... we all prey upon the weak.*

The Grillitch

Rie Sheridan Rose

"And when it's dark and rainy, like tonight," Connor murmured in a sepulchral voice, "the Grillitch roams the countryside looking for souls to eat."

Peter glanced around the tent, brown eyes wide, wringing his hands. "What does it look like?" His voice was a mere breath of sound, nearly inaudible under the susurration of the rain.

Connor rolled his eyes. "Baby! It won't come in here. Not with the lantern going. He likes the dark."

"But what does he *look* like?"

"That's what makes him so wicked," Connor said with a smirk. "No one alive has seen him. No one can describe him. He moves through the shadows, striking like lightning!" He lunged forward.

Peter screeched, fell off his camp-stool and crawled away from the other boy like a crab.

Connor laughed until tears rolled down his cheeks. "Oh, my god! I think you wet yourself," he hooted, pointing.

Peter's head came up. A curious light gleamed deep in his eyes—eyes that were now a bilious green, with pupils like a cat's. His face began to shift—planes moving forward, slipping back.

Connor stopped laughing. His brow furrowed as a puzzled frown bloomed. "What the—?"

Peter rose to his feet, towering over the older boy. "You should be grateful," he said, as thick blue fur sprouted on his face and hands, "You get to see the Grillitch for yourself." Quick as a firefly's blink he grabbed Connor by the throat. "Too bad you won't be able to tell anyone what he looks like."

The Vampire Syndrome

Olivia Arieti

In times when the vampire myth re-flourished, Damien took advantage of his resemblance to the dark creatures and diverted himself in playing such an unusual role. He had been born in a village in Eastern Europe and moved to Wittenshire when he was a child. The manor his parents purchased was lost in the countryside, surrounded by a landscape so barren that not even the wild fowls or beasts sought nourishment in its fields.

He was mostly left alone and became a bookworm which soon developed into a deep interest in the occult, black magic and the paranormal. He wished he were a wizard, able to cast evil spells on some of the servants he detested, on his schoolmates who considered him posh and haughty and even on the teachers who didn't accept his restlessness. Books about vampirism were his favourites and the bloodsuckers' mysterious darkness and heinous power intrigued him immediately.

When Allyson, the coolest girl in school, invited him to a masquerade at her villa, he had no problem in choosing his costume, Count Dracula was perfect for him. Before leaving, he contemplated his image in front of the looking glass. The innate parlour, the aristocratic lineaments, dark hair and eyes perfectly recalled the features of the renowned hellish nobleman. To add to it, his classy and reserved attitude helped to form the necessary halo of mystery typical of the species.

The girls fell for him at once and rivalry began pricking their hearts. They giggled, smiled and cast languid looks at the shadiest boy of the party. Reminiscent of the latest films they'd watched or of the stories read, they began whispering one to the other, both tremulous and wistful to utter their suspicions: Damien was a vampire.

Paradoxically, all wanted to be kissed or rather *bitten*.

While their suspicions pleased him, the advances were annoying.

Allyson smiled wickedly, "Vexed for being discovered? Why don't we take a walk in the park so you can tell me all about it?"

She took his arm and that was enough to set him on fire.

"You can start telling me how old you really are... One hundred? Two hundred, perhaps?"

"Is it so important, sweetie?" he muttered and pulled her behind the trunk of a big tree. Damien was enwrapped in its drooping branches, he held her tight and let his lips move down her face and neck.

"Bite me," Allyson said languidly, "I want to be yours forever..."

She hadn't finished talking yet when a bleak shadow clad in a midnight cloak which revealed blazing eyes pushed the boy away and plunged two sharp fangs into the girl's neck.

An inhuman cry resounded, the music stopped and all revellers dashed towards the location.

Damien was frightened and dismayed and had already run back to the ball room. The lethal presence had disappeared by the time they arrived and found Allyson agonizing at the base of the tree, her gown smeared with blood.

Great was the stupor when the doctors told the police about the two wounds in the neck that had caused the abundant outpour of blood.

No weapon was found, no evidence whatever and no explanation followed.

Damien could not figure out what happened... The girls kept glaring at him and whispers turned into horrid rumours.

Time passed, school finished and he resolved to lie low for a while. They were tormented months, his nights and days were haunted by Allyson's death and the ominous shadow. He felt observed or followed wherever he went; surely some uncanny presence was lurking somewhere in the endless corridors and huge halls... someone who, for some unknown reason, was after him.

More than a year had elapsed when he bumped into Allyson's cousin, Edith, who cried, "You may outfox the police, but not me. I know you're a bloodsucker, we all know it and look what you've done to Allyson."

"Why don't you come to my house? Then I'll tell you all about it." He cast a lustful glance at the girl.

Curious and enticed like the others by his obscure charm, Edith promised to visit him.

Her words disturbed Damien. He ran home and went into the library; searching among the many old volumes until he found one concerning the family history. He whitened on reading that there had been more than a vampire among his ancestors...

Could he be one as well? Once again he went through his books on vampirism and as he continued reading, more and more he believed to be one.

Edith and her friends were right.

Maybe, he was just a beginner and still had to develop the most hideous features of his ancestors. Soon he would no longer see his image reflected anywhere and the thirst for blood would force him to awful deeds. Surely, all powers would come after his first bite.

He had to find out quickly and at that moment the the image of his potential victim flashed before him.

That evening Edith was at the manor.

His parents were abroad and only the housekeeper was there.

A thick fog had arisen and the place looked grim, almost scary. Edith shuddered as she walked carefully through the gate, but was determined to find proofs for all suspicions.

She was no longer an adolescent, she had grown into a seductive young lady, one unable to conceal her anxiety. She looked extremely vulnerable to his piercing eyes.

Damien offered her a drink and, although they were both a bit nervous, they started an amiable conversation about the old school days till they suddenly silenced.

The moment to face the matter had arrived.

"So you believe I'm a vampire," Damien said dryly.

Edith nodded.

"Aren't you scared? Or are you planning to take out some garlic and mustard seeds to frighten me away?"

"Not scared enough to decline your invitation," she replied provocatively.

"Allyson begged me to bite her... perhaps, you want it too?" he asked, picking up the challenge in her tone.

"I just want to learn the truth."

"That's the only way you'll find out, my dear."

A sudden attraction seized him, her breath was inebriating and he moved closer to her.

"Prove that you're not afraid, darling. A little bite can't hurt you..."

Edith kept gazing at him as though hypnotized by his voice and he wondered if his eyes had turned red...

He began caressing her curls and slowly pushed them back, leaving her long neck visible... His throat wasn't dry, though, and the teeth weren't piercing his tongue, but he didn't care and kissed her passionately.

Whilst Edith was living the part of the wretched heroine about to be ravished by her shady villain, Damien only wanted to satisfy his lewd appetite.

She, too, begged to be bitten.

His pleasure was darkened by the dreadful shadow lurking in the corner of the room.

Was it planning to harm Edith as well?

"You have to go, darling, but I'll come for you," he said and felt obliged to add, "I like the taste of your blood."

Still entranced by his touch, Edith left her lover, unable to figure out his true nature. She hoped he would call her again or visit her in the intimacy of her own room, careless if he drained all her blood; desire had kindled her more than horror and she was dying to be his again.

Once alone, Damien rushed in front of the mirror and the image of a scoundrel sneered back at him. His teeth showed no change and the only drink he yearned for was some strong whisky to wash away the bitter taste of blood still in his mouth.

All evidence proved he wasn't a vampire.

He was disappointed at being denied such a privilege, he cursed and damned all supernatural creatures and his foolishness for not realising that his family history was full of stupid fantasies and false veracities.

Whatever, his role diverted him and he decided to carry on the farce.

He became depraved and wicked and many other heroines, dressed in black and with claw-like fingernails, wanted to become the dark lord's bride.

The encounters always ended with a bite that, even if totally disgusting, was due to his victims.

The shadow appeared rarely and he soon persuaded himself that it was nothing but an eerie hallucination.

As happens with all trends, appeal and excitement soon vanished and Damien got tired of his role. His casual lovers had turned doubtful. Since he never visited them and they didn't grow weak or cadaverous, they soon looked forward to new affairs.

Only the twilight walks through the park weren't abandoned; the ghastly penumbra, the rising mist that like a soft chill entered his skin and appeased his senses. On one of those occasions, he met Melanie. She sat weeping on a bench, wrapped in an oversize black coat. Toying with her long raven hair.

"Is there anything I can do, Miss?" he asked, almost timidly.

"No, Sir, it's just that I can't get over it."

Her crimson lips stirred his desire at once.

She told him an ordinary story about her fiancé walking out on her and began sobbing again. Somehow she resembled Allyson, the only girl Damien had really cared for.

He gently took her hand and held it till she stopped weeping.

"I'm so sorry to have burdened you with my grief," she said and fixed her eyes on his. Her glance mesmerised him.

"I don't live far from here... Would you like a drink?"

"I'd love to learn more about the bastard who left you in such a state," he replied hastily.

Shortly afterwards, Damien was in Melanie's living room.

The room was dark and damp as though the curtains had never been drawn.

His hostess lit a few candles; instead if brightening up the room made it look gloomier, almost funereal. She told him she lived there alone; her parents passed away many years ago and also her sister had died young. Probably her tight smiles were due to the grief she had gone through. The tone was low, often intermitted by sighs and now and then a tear rolled down her pale cheeks.

For the first time, he was seized by tenderness and compassion.

For him, spending the evening together wasn't enough, he wanted to see her again.

Melanie, too, had been attracted by his handsome features and more encounters followed.

Although Damien had totally fallen for her, there was something about their relationship that disturbed him; quite often she was detached, didn't show up when expected and was never available till late afternoon. He attributed her behaviour to her past losses, to the fear of being forsaken again. The best way to assure her of his feelings was to marry her and a few months later he proposed.

"I want you to be mine forever," he said as he gave her a ruby ring, one of the family's jewels, "I cannot think of my life without you, darling."

Melanie gazed at him and the evil twinkle in her eyes didn't go unnoticed. Then she looked at the ring... the gem was as red as a drop of fresh blood.

"Just what I wished, love," she muttered. Instead of kissing him, she dug her sparkling fangs into his neck.

"What the heck are you doing?" he cried, bewildered.

"Why so upset? We'll always be together and share the horrors of darkness for all the years to come."

Damien glared at her; he felt weaker and weaker and his throat was burning more than hell... This time he wanted blood, glasses full of that crimson fluid he'd do anything to get.

"You bloody bitch," he shouted, "you've ruined me!"

"Why, honey? I simply made your wish come true... besides, there're bright sides to being vampires, trust me."

"*Bright* sides, huh?" he sneered. "So you were that shadow that kept haunting me, the one that killed Allyson?"

Melanie now smiled and made visible her fangs still tinged with blood. "I had set my eyes on you and wanted you for myself."

After cursing the vampire, Damien rushed home and stood in front of the mirror, only to see that no image was reflected.

He began pacing the floor; his weakness and dismay slowly giving way to an unfamiliar morbid craving that urged him to search for prey as fast as possible.

Ironically, he had reassumed his role.
A few minutes later, he was calling on Edith.

174

Acid Queen

Dan Allen

This is another goddamn hangover. Where am I? Hard, cold, musty. Basement floor? How did I get here? This one's a doozy, alright. What happened to my nose? Did I get punched? Probably fell - again. I really need to stop drinkin'. Hope it's not busted... Wait... what the hell is on my foot? It looks like... blood. Shit, something chewed off my toe or... maybe it's melted. There's a puddle under my foot. Wish I could see it better. It smells bad, toxic, like chemicals. Damn, I'm dizzy. might need to sleep this off a bit longer.

***

"Alice? Is that you, baby? I need some help."

I must still be drunk. Looks like she's wearing a gas mask.

"What happened to me last night? Are you not going to tell? Do you know where my clothes are?

"Hush. One question for you, Asshole. Do you see?"

I don't understand her. I never really have.

"Are you pissed at me or something? Hey, what's in the jug? Muriatic acid? What the hell, Allie. Be careful with that stuff. No! Don't pour it on my feet! Quick, get water and wash it off."

Whoa... wait a minute. What's with the syringe?

"Alice, honey, you know I don't like needles. No, don't do it. Please, Allie, not in the neck...

Spinning, turning, Alice's face revolving around me. Faster, I'm drifting, falling, slipping into the dark.

"Why are you doing this? Why?"

***

It's morning. Sunlight flooding the room, burning through my eyelids. Heat on my forehead and inside my brain, not from the sun. I'm fevered, sweat's trickling into my eyes. It's stinging, I can't move my arms. Can't feel anything below my neck.

"Do you see?"

She's yelling at me now, telling me to wake up. Screw her. I'm pretending to sleep. She slaps my face once, twice, grabs a handful of hair and lifts my head.

"Look."

Alice is pointing... my foot boils with a million tiny white bubbles. They're jumping and popping and sizzling and... my foot is dissolving! Toes are still there; white, cleaned of flesh... the rest is a gory mess of ligaments, cartilage and pink mush. This should hurt. Why don't I feel any pain? The injections, of course. Duh. Alice grabs my neck and squeezes. I should spit on her, show her I'm still boss. Might be my only chance. But, I listen and she's whispering. Her voice is seductive, breath warm and, for a moment, I mistakenly think she might save me.

"It would be a shame if you died now. I have so much more work to do."

Alice licks my cheek, reaches for the gas mask, slips it on and morphs into an alien. I'm high, hallucinating, wasted. What's in the syringe? Something that paralyzes... some kind of narcotic. The jug of muriatic acid appears; she's dribbling some over my shins, calves and one enormous drop on my thigh.

"Just a little, right, Asshole? One for the road? We wouldn't want the fun to end too soon, would we?"

I see the needle. Wow, I'm spinning already. She must've upped the dose. I'm going to kill her. Yes, that's what I'm going to do, soon as I get out of here. Strangle the bitch. Laughing? Do I hear her laughing? Why is she laughing? What's so funny...

***

"Open your eyes. I know you're awake."

Oh, yes, Alice. Love of my life. How could I forget? She's behind me, I feel her hands slide through my hair, under my ears, against my cheekbones.

"Sit up, asshole."

She jerks on my head, forces my shoulders off the ground. She tugs again. Any harder and the bitch will decapitate me.

"Do you see?"

My legs are foaming and alive with activity. My drugged-out mind finds it fascinating, but no, this is

177

my flesh dissolving and I scream. Alice punches me hard in my temple, just above my left ear.

"Shut up and look."

I open my eyes. A coin-sized hole in my thigh spews pink foam, like a tiny volcano erupting melted flesh. I know that spot and I remember a droplet landing there. I risk looking at my lower legs. A patchwork of smouldering acid splotches burn through the remaining tissue.

Farther down, my ankles and feet... They're clean and white, like the plastic skeleton we hang on Halloween. It's disgusting. How will I walk? A black curtain falls and I'm falling too...

***

I'm gasping, choking, sucking in a breath. There's a needle sticking out of my chest much larger than the ones before. Alice sees me looking at it.

"Adrenalin. I need you awake for this one."

The gas mask comes out again. I see a swamp monster this time and the beast is twisting the cap off a new jug. Careless splashing over my decimated lower legs, thighs, even some on my balls. The beast fills my belly button hole, closes the jug and pulls off the mask.

"Please, Alice. Please. Not my testicles. I don't know what I did, but I'm sorry. God knows I'm sorry."

I think the bitch is smiling. I'm not sure. My vision is blurry and my eyes are full of tears, or maybe it's toxic fumes.

178

"Do you see now, Asshole? Do you see?"

"No, I don't freaking see."

She's leaning over me, closer now. Maybe she's going to bite my nose. I wouldn't put it past her. I close my eyes. I'm not going to give her the pleasure of seeing fear. Something brushes my cheek, my lips. Did she just kiss me?

"There's no needle this time. I want you lucid. I want you to experience it all, baby."

"Go to hell."

Go to hell? Is that the best I can do? There's clicking on the wooden stairs, high heels? Is she going out? She can't leave me like this!

"Wait, Alice, come back!"

Halloween Party

SJ Townend

The last of the tallow candles had been lit and placed carefully inside a hollowed gourd. She tipped the burlap sack to check there were no more wax lights inside and, satisfied that this task at least was fulfilled, tossed it empty to the ground. Hands on hips, she looked out and down at her work; a myriad of glowing grins encircled her ranch house, all evil eyes, staring outwards, ready to greet her guests.

The hint of ink in the sky told her it was nearly time. All those she'd zealously invited would surely be soon to arrive so she turned around with haste and made her way back up to the house to carry on with the rest of her preparations. Left foot in front of right and caught up in the wonderment of which guests would be first to arrive, she lost track of her footing—her hobnailed boot caught under an old tree root. She stumbled and fell. She cursed the gnarled tree, which was older than the farmhouse itself, brushed the dry soil from her tatty tea dress and stood up. The pain in her toe throbbed, then trickled away like leaves rolling off with the wind and the furled trunk of the tree appeared to grimace down.

She'd invited them all, the entire town which her ranch house looked down on. Some were close friends and family, some she hadn't seen for years, some she'd never been introduced to but had bumped into during a dark night on the way home from the tavern. Each bloody invitation had felt just right.

She considered her progress with the party preparations and almost a smile lifted the apples of her sallow cheeks. She'd done a good job with the bonfire. It'd torn the tissues in her back to shreds, lugging and stacking the stinking fuel it would need to get it blazing, but she felt it'd been worth it. She was proud of her accomplishments.

She had been raised by her Grandfather—who'd passed a year earlier—and had never known much of praise from others, nor kindness in any form and had learned to bestow such praise and validation on herself or go without.

Her cruel Grandfather had told her many dark tales, but the best of a bad bunch had been the story of All Hallow's Eve. The year before, a few days before he died, he'd told her in a haze of whisky malice the story of how the souls of the dead returned on All Hallows' Day to visit their families, to embrace them, to ask for forgiveness, or to settle up. Tonight she'd wait and see if Grandfather's tale reeked of truth.

A single tear, clearing a pathway through the grime on her cheek, rolled down her face as she thought of the mean old man. She wiped the tear away and stood tall; looking at the stack she'd built. *What a fabulous pyre,* she thought. *It'll go up a treat.* The tear was one of joy.

Her hands bled with her own blood, sore from the scraping and carving of over a hundred jack-o-lanterns. Each lantern was now lit with a candle, each lantern a memory of an individual—a glowing lamp for each of those she'd invited, each of those she'd crept up behind over the year that had been and gone. There was one flickering orange face for each of those whose throats she'd cut. Crimson mingled with dirt and mania now, staining her cheeks, owning her face as she pushed her dirty hair from her eyes.

She set about slicing the oranges, grating the cinnamon, uncorking the bottles of red. She poured the last of the liquor and other special ingredients she'd gathered from empty townhouses into the vat in which she'd mull the wine. After this, she only had the apples to clean and set to float in the cattle trough. There'd been a time, before Grandfather died, when she'd find great solace amidst the silence of the water trough. She'd submerge her whole body, clamp her nose and mouth closed with her hand, hold her breath for as long as she could to remain in the icy void. There, her tears found a new home. *The apples will make the trough more fun for my guests,* she thought, *especially the ones writhing with maggots.*

If none of them came back from wherever the dead go, if no-one returned so she could kill them all again, she swore she'd join them on the other side on the morrow and catch them all there. With a lifeless terrain of spent farmland, dust, more dust and nothing but locusts, with no body left to take down, what joy was there left for her alive?

She sat back in her rocking chair out on the porch and waited. Back and forth she rocked; her lost eyes flitted between her broken skin, the oozing wounds on her tired palms and the path leading up to her party.

She waited until she was certain. Certain that no-one was going to come. Until Hallows' Eve rolled into Hallows' Day, until midnight came and went. Until her eyelids started to fall down as heavily as the thud an old man makes when hitting cobblestones, when slit fresh a red Cheshire cat smile.

I guess they're not coming back, she thought. She stared at the mass of burning bodies, her soul, a deflated balloon. She stood up from her chair and set about her final task.

***

The eternal sun rose above its green blanket, shone with a muffled glow as it would the following day and the day after that. The bonfire: a heap of glowing embers, charred bones and blackened teeth. The mulled wine: cold, congealed. The hollowed pumpkins were vacant of light and life, now only rotten, hollowed fruit, food for no thing. As the planet spun onwards—as it would do forever, turning to face and then to escape once more the ball of fire in the sky—a new length of shadow grew and grew, all the shape of a young lady, noose for a necklace, draped from the cursed tree of Old Maple Farm.

Lawn Care

Rickey Rivers Jr.

Forgive me. I overslept. I set the alarm. It's raining now. The weather man predicted rain. The yard needs to be cut. It's damp. Now I have to wait for the sun. I have to trim it down, keep it tame. Ask Ms. Bennington. She knows why. Last time it grew too tall and snatched up her cat. She hasn't forgiven me.

Taming any living thing is nearly impossible. Some people can't even tame their children, much less pets. There's only so much time in the day and it grows so fast. One lawn can't survive off water alone. You understand. We all have to work. I come home tired and the neighbors ask the same ole thing "When're you cutting the grass?"

Then I have to response with the same old thing, a smile and a wave or just "Any day now."

The 'any day now' is true. It always happens any day I can actually do it, any day the lawn lets me, any day the lawn isn't so wet. I'm not purposely letting it grow so much. Judgment from the neighbors certainly doesn't help. I hear whispers all the time.

"Why doesn't she just cut the grass?"

Like it's so simple, like it doesn't grow four times as fast, like it doesn't crave the taste of meat.

I don't control the yard. I don't know why they think I can. I don't have powers. I just sometimes dream of the yard snatching them out of their homes, pulling them out, ripping every person to shreds. Then there'd be reason to complain. Alas, a home owner has to deal with such manners. None of these people pay the bills here. Yet they complain and complain, day after day.

When the rain stops I'll cut the yard. Everything'll go back to normal. Until the rain starts again, then the yard will be hungry. I can almost sense how it feels. It loves the rain. When I was a child I loved the rain too. But I got older, bitter. I'm sick of the rain now. The yard needs it, but it always needs more, wants more and more. Water's good, but we know what it likes the most.

Only a while longer before the rain stops. Then I'll give it a trim. It hates when I cut too low, have to cut it just right. The lawn is a selfish sod, the most selfish. And my neighbors think the same of me, funny.

I pity their children most of all, having to outrun or out-bike the tendrils, must be terrible. Back in the day children would gladly cut lawns for a bit of change but children these days are lazy or scared or both; who I kidding? I don't blame them.

Parents can't even control them. If one were taken I know who they'd blame.

"Tame that lawn!" they'd say.

"Control the weeds!" they'd holler.

"Control your children!" I'd holler back.

Everything's much easier said than done. People don't control children or pets or even their own lives. They worry about control over others. They worry when something happens to them. It's not my fault you all suck.

I too grow tired of cutting the lawn. I too grow tired of living here. They don't understand or care to understand. All they have to do is go to work, come home and maybe cut their lawns every two weeks. They get dinner with family, barbeques, the whole shebang, free from stress, free from worry, or care. They don't even invite me over.

Why would they? They don't care. They only care that I'm here and cutting the grass. That's all I'm worth. I'm a landscaper. It's like I don't even own the home. I pay bills for the right to live. The lawn owns the home. The neighbors knew that when I moved in. They're all in on it. They've always been.

I can't protect this neighborhood, not anymore. I just can't do it. I've put up caution signs in the past. They've been eaten. I try to hire professional landscapers and they get scared to death and nearly eaten. It's out of control. It's no way to live.

I should take a vacation. Then what? Then the lawn would really get out of hand. The weeds would grow toward the street like tentacles stretching out. Soon those weeds would reach other homes. Soon their door handles. Children would leave home and never return. They'd be caught, the weeds soon wrapping around their throats. Mommy and Daddy would run over to complain and without a sound the yard would swallow them up too.

Oh, Ms. Bennington, you can see your cat again. Be reunited now, all ye to hell. Goodbye neighborhood watch. So long, girl scouts. Thanks for the cookies. Let the lawn swallow you whole. I don't care anymore. I hope it rains forever. Let the lawn take my home. I won't need it. I'll be a caretaker no more. Dying can't be worse than servitude.

Maybe the neighbors will thank me for saving them from their boring suburban lifestyle. Wouldn't that be something?

"You're welcome!" I'd say. It's been a pleasure to serve you. I'll see you beneath it all, in the after, after we serve the lawn from below. Let the rain bring peace, happiness and everything that comes with an untamed lawn. I dare say I welcome the change. I'm ready for the grass on the other side. It'll be greener, greater.

The Great Lesson

R.G. Evans

These are the woods, he thought. *The very woods*.

Cox's woods.

He turned off the ignition and climbed out of the pickup into the heat of an unseasonably warm October afternoon. He looked up at the wall of trees--oaks, maples, a few birches and hollies--a magnificent nebula of oranges, golds and reds. He breathed in a lungful of Indian summer and thought of old man Cox who used to own these woods. Surely he'd be dead after all these years.

I wonder if he suffered at the end, he thought.

He walked around to the rear of the truck, lowered the tailgate and heaved the canvas duffel bag over his shoulder. It was only a few short steps from where the dirt road ended and the woods began. He entered the shady grove and felt the day's heat disappear. It was like stepping into a wholly different day. Like going back in time.

He gazed up into the canopy and remembered how the trees had teemed with squirrels that day he and his father had come to Cox's woods.

His father had never been a great man. Small in stature. Soft spoken. And yet his father had been the man who taught him the Great Lesson--and he had taught it right here among these trees.

He remembered the way his father carried his Winchester twelve gauge over his forearm, barrels pointed toward the ground. He remembered looking up at his father, seeing his black and red CPO coat and neon orange hunting cap. He remembered how he held one finger to his lips, the way the shotgun's barrels raised slowly like the railroad crossing gate at Cooch's Bridge Road. He followed those rising barrels with his gaze until they pointed up into the treetops then roared like fiery thunder.

It echoed in his ears, but not enough to drown out the sound of a small body plummeting through the leaves.

His father led him to where the squirrel had fallen and when they looked down, they both saw that it was still alive, riddled with shot and bleeding, twitching as if it had been electrocuted.

And the sound. A high-pitched keen of pain and terror he remembered to this day.

"Poor little fella," his father had said, picking up the squirrel by its tail and swinging it skull first into the bole of an oak.

Another sound he'd never forget.

When the squirrel's skull crunched against that tree, he'd felt as if his own skull had cracked open like an egg, the hatchling of a monumental truth filling his mind with light.

Death was not pain or something to be feared. Death was *release* from pain.

Death was beautiful.

And that beauty had been brought forth by his father's hands.

Now, he breathed in the day's cool fecundity and moved deeper into the woods, the crackle of leaves making a soothing rhythm. He shifted the canvas bag on his shoulder.

The Great Lesson had shown him the way. He remembered the starling trapped inside their garage days later. He'd fired off at least a dozen rounds with his BB gun before one winged the bird and it flopped to the floor. How light it was when he picked it up, its delicate hollow bones. How he squeezed it slowly, slowly.

Until it was beautiful.

Rabbits he'd snare. Kittens he'd lure with cans of tuna. The neighbors' aged dog. All of them rungs on the ladder leading from the Great Lesson to ever higher perches of beauty.

He stopped. Just ahead of him stood a great oak, acorns littering the ground, all little bodies that had plunged from above. He couldn't be sure this was the spot, but it felt right.

He shrugged the bag off his shoulder and laid it gently on the forest floor.

His father had never been a great man. Soft spoken, even more so as the illness had progressed through a body so slight of stature that it had fit easily into the canvas duffle bag.

When he unzipped the bag, a gasp came from within.

The cancer had turned his father into an emaciated mannequin, a doll with parchment skin and bones that might as well have been as hollow as a bird's. He bent down and lifted the frail body out of the bag and laid it down on the leaves. His father wheezed painfully, his eyes rolling in their sockets, unable to focus.

He bent down and took a firm grip on both of his father's stick-like ankles. He looked at the oak.

"Poor little fella," he said.

And swung.

The Others

Joseph J Dowling

Underneath the vast, shattered city, the others cowered—third and fourth generation blind, their mutated genes passed down after the bomb. Above, in the brutal and endless nuclear winter, as the repeating process of survive, repair, survive continued, fragile society tried to ignore the sightless horror lurking below.

***

I turned to Akiro. His lank, greasy hair covered his face as he worked on the crumbling engine block.

"Hurry up, man!" I urged, stomping my frozen feet.

"Chill out, Hachiro, I'm going as fast as I can," he said as he continued stripping out the rusted spark plugs and any other salvageable parts from the bones of an ancient Toyota. Well, I knew it was a Toyota—to most, it was just a junked wreck from before the war. Akiro groaned with immense effort. "Gimmie a hand over here, this last one's a son of a bitch." I ran over, scanning the decrepit old mechanic's yard. "Got it!" he cried in triumph as the last plug came with a cranking squeal, thanks to the extra leverage.

My strained voice echoed tightly off the cracked concrete.   "Let's get out of here." Something wasn't right about this place. Despite the thin layer of ice which blanketed everything, it smelled damp and musty, almost rotten, like it wanted to be forgotten.

***

Below, two of them easily followed the sounds of the above dwellers as they worked, moved, and talked.   Their   perspiration   sent   waves   of pheromones through the stale air. The two men were strong and healthy, but food was scarce, opportunities few. They would need to split the men up and they would need to attack quickly, otherwise they would fail and they would all starve.

***

A metallic *clang* came from the other side of the Toyota as something heavy fell. Fear clawed at me and my voice rose by several pitches. "What the hell was that?" Akiro spun, coiled and ready. A few seconds passed and nothing moved.

"I'll check it out. You stay here and keep your eyes open." He inched towards the spot where the sound came from, hunched down and alert. Akiro always was the brave one. He wiped his face with his tattered shirt sleeve as his blade slid out from its sheath with a silent whisper.

"See anything?" I said, craning around to look in all directions at once. I leaned around the Toyota to follow him as he edged forward.

"It's a socket wrench. Must've fallen from somewhere." He bent down to pick it up with his spare hand, tucking it into his overall. "This'll come in han—" Suddenly there was movement and a grey flash of limbs. Akiro cried out as it clawed at him. Another joined in from behind, pulling at his long hair while I froze, briefly paralysed by shock.

"Help me!" he cried. My friend's shout was enough to pull me out of fear induced incapacitation and I dashed towards the tangle of bodies. My foot dragged and I fell. Tumbling, I caught sight of a grey wrist snaking back into the shadows. There were three of them now—at *least* three.

I looked up as Akiro plunged the blade into the midriff of one of his attackers. When he pulled it out, there was a sickly sucking sound, like a stick from thick mud and the thing emitted an inhuman, high-pitched shriek. Without hesitation, Akiro shivved the sharp blade into the stunned creature's throat as it bent double. Arterial blood jetted out of the small, ragged tear.

There was a glint of metal as the second creature wildly flailed at him and a damp thud as a metal bar struck Akiro's back. He cried out in pain and fell forward, stumbling but keeping his balance, but only just. His blade clattered to the floor, skidding out of reach.

The third one was still in the shadows, lurking like a rat in a drainpipe, waiting for a chance to catch me unawares. I ran the other way around the car as Akiro struggled, winded. I had no weapon so I launched myself and my forearm smashed into the side of the thing's head. It snarled, lashing out. Long fingernails sliced across my face. I could hear a scurrying sound as the third one took its chance, but by the time it came at us, Akiro had recovered his blade and had the creature's pal by its grey, sloping forehead. He sliced the knife across its soft, white, exposed neck. Blood gushed out in a waterfall and it slumped straight down, cross-legged, like a drunk in a doorway.

"Duck!" he cried, raising the wrench he had picked up earlier. I threw myself to the floor. Our connection was almost telepathic after so many years scavenging together and I knew what he wanted to do. The wrench flew straight and true, spinning end over end, and struck the thing above the eye with a strangled *clunk*. The sightless creature howled and reeled, sensing the attack had failed and its comrades lay dead. It tried to turn and run, but I grabbed its leg and pulled it over. *How do you like it the other way around, bitch?!*

Akiro came towards it, striding with intent. He kneeled on its chest and it made sad, whimpering sounds as it lay helpless under the weight. I could almost hear it pleading *I'm sorry, it won't happen again. We're just so... so hungry!* For the first time, I had a clear and uninterrupted look at one of them. It was slick and hairless, with blank white eyes redundant in deeply hollowed sockets. Puffs of condensation rose with each ragged breath. Its irritated, irradiated lungs rasped and wheezed, with no medicine to heal them. I almost felt sorry for it. *Almost*.

"Do it," I urged as Akiro held the blade aloft, in both fists, aimed precisely at where the thing's rapidly beating heart must be. But then he slowly lowered the knife.

"I got a better idea," he said. "Throw me that cord from your pack." I did nothing, unsure of his intensions, before I slowly understood his plan.

"You're insane, Akiro. We can't bring that thing back with us. The rest of the group will freak out, man! Besides, who knows what diseases they carry?"

"Just hand me the damn rope," he ordered. I acquiesced. There was no point arguing with Akiro when he'd made up his mind. While other members of our group didn't, I instinctively knew when to push him and when not—one of the many reasons we worked so well together. Such a lot of egos and alpha dogs in our crew, but I usually preferred to play a supporting role and follow orders.

His quick fingers soon had the thing hogtied. It emitted a slow, sad groan. I could sense its sensitive mind grappling with its fate, senses overstimulated, unused to spending so long above ground.

"Let's bounce, before its friends come," Akiro said as he pulled the thing up onto its feet, which were the same grey as the endless, snow-flecked skies looming above, visible through the yard's cracked canopy. It stood quietly, with its head bowed, radiating apprehension like ripples in a lake. This time, I felt a jolt of real sympathy.

***

In the sewer below, several of them huddled, listening. The men had been too strong, too healthy. They could not risk their numbers dwindling further and waited in impotent anguish for the men to leave so they could recover the corpses. At least they would not go hungry today.

***

Back at the warehouse, our group stood in silence, surrounding the thing in a rough semi-circle as it sat, bound to a grimy, moss covered plastic chair, in turn shackled to a long-seized up radiator. Its head lolled, given in to its fate.

Daichi stared at it, his finger and thumb resting against his chin, which was covered in a closely cropped beard, speckled with white. His deep voice boomed in the vast, empty building, causing the captive to flinch at the harsh sound.

"Doc, check this thing over. Perhaps we can learn something. I mean, these freaks were like us, what, eighty or so years ago, right?"

Doc ran forward and snapped on some blue gloves. He knelt and examined his subject, feeling for its blinking pulse and shining his tiny torch deep into those white, sightless eyes.

Perhaps Daichi was right. Maybe we could figure out how to live side-by-side with the others. If we could save the four of five human lives we lost every year to their attacks, it would be worth it. We'd all seen enough slaughter to last a thousand

197

epochs. This city was big enough for us, the rats *and* this Godforsaken species, surely?

Tunnel of Love

Rie Sheridan Rose

The air seemed almost alive—redolent with the sweet scents of kettle corn and cotton candy. Screams and laughter from the rides surrounding the midway helped the impression of the air living with their cacophony of sound. Strolling patrons, snapping flags, glittering lights—everything meshed together in a dizzying world of excitement where anything might lie around the next corner.

Barkers called from their colorful tents, battling to be heard over the calliope music pumping out onto the carnival from hidden speakers.

"Come see the two-headed boy!"

"This way to the bearded lady."

"The mysterious Orient has nothing on the sights we have for you!"

Gillian shivered with excitement, clutching Trevor's arm tightly. "What should we do first? It's all so... big, and brassy, and... oh, Trev, it's wonderful!"

Trevor looked down at the girl with a fond, amused smile and patted her hand. "Don't worry, Gilly. We have plenty of time to see it all. You pick. What do you want to do first?"

A becoming blush painted her cheeks scarlet as she pointed toward one of the rides looming beside the midway. "Can we do that?"

He cocked an eyebrow at the suggestion. "You want to go through the Tunnel of Love?"

"Yes, please," she whispered, looking up at him through her lashes.

"You sure?"

She nodded, ducking her head. They hadn't been dating long and she was being very forward, but she just couldn't help herself. He was absolutely perfect for her.

Trevor chuckled. "Aren't you the impetuous one?" He led her over to the ticket booth. "Two tickets please, my good man."

The attendant grinned from ear to ear, showing off a bright gold incisor. "Looks like we have a pair of lovebirds out of their nest tonight. Well, we'll lend you one of ours. Right this way to the ride of your life!" He shepherded them through a series of switchback ropes until they were at the embarkation spot for the ride.

Gillian looked around, a slight frown wrinkling her brow. "There's no line."

"We've been set up here a week, little lady. Most everyone who wants to cuddle in the dark has ridden it already and any new riders tend to come right at the end of the night. Think of this as a private trip." He winked at her.

"Oh. Okay…"

Trevor helped her into the garishly painted swan car and took a seat beside her. The attendant pulled down the safety bar and locked it in place.

"Enjoy your ride!" he caroled as he went back to his control panel. He pushed a button and music began to swell out of the ride. It was an odd, slightly off-key melody that set Gillian's teeth on edge.

She turned to Trevor. "Something's not right. I... I've changed my mind, Trevor. I want to get off."

"It's too late for that. We're moving."

The car was indeed gliding up the rising track toward the mouth of the Tunnel of Love. Only now did Gillian notice the entrance was a *literal* mouth—the heart-shaped opening framed by the painted lips for some monstrous Cupid decorating the side of the ride.

"It's awful! Why would anyone put a painting like that on a ride that's supposed to be—"

"—Supposed to be what, Gilly? Y'know what they say, 'love is a many splendored thing.' Maybe this is someone else's idea of love."

An icy wind blew through the building, and she shivered. "It's certainly not *my* idea of love."

"Oh? And what were you expecting? Fat cherubic archers and shiny red hearts? How clichéd. I rather like this—it's unexpected, and exciting."

A spotlight clicked on, revealing a robed figure holding aloft what looked like a dripping human heart.

"That's not love! What the hell is this place?"

"Of course it's love. The sacrifice gave his life because of his love for his people and the priest offers up the heart for the love of his gods."

"It's cruel and ghastly. I want to go home. Stop the ride at once!"

"Things don't work like that, Gillian. We can't just get off now. We have to ride to the conclusion. Remember—this was *your* idea."

She sobbed, "I hate it!"

Another spotlight flashed on. This time it illuminated a pair of dogs rutting. The chamber filled with the sounds of canine copulation.

"That's disgusting!"

"Why? It's all part of nature."

"B-but it isn't nice. Especially on a ride where there might be children!"

"Didn't you see the sign? 'Ages 18 and up.' It was right by the ticket booth."

"I want to go home, Trevor. As soon as we get off this ride."

He slipped an arm around her shoulders and pulled her to him. "If that's what you truly want. But remember, you asked for this."

She tried to pull away, but he held her tight. "T-Trevor...what are you doing?"

"This is the Tunnel of Love, isn't it? I'm just showing you how much you mean to me."

Another flash of light hit Gillian directly in the eyes. "W-What is going on? I'm not part of this!"

She turned toward him.

"Of course you are, darling," Trevor murmured. He grinned widely, exposing sharply-pointed fangs. "Let me show you how much I love you, Gillian." He bent toward her, the deadly fangs glistening in the spotlight.

Gillian screamed.

***

202

Outside the ride, the attendant flipped a sign to "Closed for Maintenance." He shook his head indulgently, quirking his finger at one of the roustabouts. "Clean up in Aisle Six again, Billy."

The boy grinned and shook his head as he fetched a mop and pail.

The ride attendant sighed. "Someday the Boss'll learn to curb his appetites, I guess. If he don't, we'll run out of states to play in." He gave a sharp whistle and the other carnies looked over at his booth.

"Time to pack up," he called to the rest of the carnies. "The Tunnel's overflowed again."

One by one, the midway lights went out.

Deadly Knots

Olivia Arieti

The weather promised nothing good and Captain Frederick was worried. Many were the knots they still had to sail and the autumn winds were already whistling menacingly. The seadog knew the first storms were the worst, always anxious to prevaricate and depose the previous season. His three-masted merchant ship was getting old and, eager to reach the home port as fast as possible, he feared that something might go wrong. On board was the gorgeous Lady Caroline Carson, the bride to be of his closest friend, Earl Joseph Westville. Her father, Count Carson, was more an adventurer than a nobleman and after betrothing the girl to his cousin's heir, he crossed the ocean with his family and settled down in an overseas country where he carried on his business and zest for exploration. The promise was that on Caroline's eighteenth birthday he would send her back for the wedding.

With endless tears for leaving her dearest and being thrust into unknown arms, Caroline boarded the ship with her maidservant, Alisa, a pretty lass who, unlike her mistress, was thrilled and excited about the new adventure.

The crew was made of poor sailors hardened by life at sea and once they caught a glimpse of the maidens, their dreams at night were no longer the same. While the countess lowered her eyes, Alisa felt flattered by their lustful glances, especially by the young officers, who quickly began competing for her favours.

The ladies were assigned two different cabins and every possible comfort was assured. In the evening they dined at the captain's table where Caroline did her best to conceal her sadness. Her charm and beauty had intrigued Frederick to the point that only the sight of her made him shudder with an unfamiliar desire.

While more than one officer had made his way through to Alisa's cabin, the noble lady was always alone and quite often he would find her on the main deck, her glance lost in the watery depths.

"You don't look too enthusiastic," he said, discerning a teardrop rolling down her cheek.

"Would you be happy to marry a complete stranger and live in a land that is no longer your own?"

"I can assure you that Earl Joseph is a most distinguished and caring fellow; he certainly will be a good husband to you."

Somehow his words sounded untrustworthy even to himself. Unpleasant rumours about the gentleman's integrity had reached him during his last stay in London; he couldn't help wondering if the guy had really turned so depraved.

Caroline smiled tightly; his words didn't convince her either.

***

Days were long at sea and nights even more so. Seeing each other on the deck had become a rendezvous and both the captain and his lovely passenger looked forward to it. Neither was Caroline indifferent to the brawny seadog's glances and soon she too was stirred by his same desire. They smiled and sighed, letting the briny gusts caress their faces while their eyes kept searching one another's, hopeful and at the same time fearful to learn the true reason for the throbbing of their hearts.

The violence of the weather apparently animated the crew's spirits and passions who too often indulged in unrestrained merriment in the attempt to dispel the terror of being swallowed by the abyss.

One evening Alisa's cry overwhelmed their boisterous laughter and tainted the night with horror; she was found in a pool of blood, atrociously stabbed by the betrayed boatswain who was still cursing and crying by her side.

When the corpse was launched into the water, the maddened man jumped after it and both became prey to the rabid sharks already skirting the ship.

The event was perceived as a bad omen and the swearing and hollow cries still echoed in the nights that followed. The girl's shadow haunted the mariners who grew tense and restless and replaced whatever mirth they had with heavy drinking. Everyone was sure that the ship was cursed, except the captain, who had never believed in silly superstitions.

The voyage had become a true torment for Caroline, now also devastated by Alisa's horrible death. Loneliness and dread for her future drove her closer to Frederick who did his best to comfort her.

On a most stormy evening, he invited her to his cabin.

The lantern's light glowed on her face and made the eyes glimmer; the lips were slightly trembling as though afraid to disclose and say what would be forever regretted... He watched her, feverish as malediction for his craving and clemency, for his weakness invested the burning soul. No battle was fought with more ardour or fear, a pungent struggle between heart and senses with conscience, the judge. In the attempt to quench his fever, he stepped away ...

When he turned round, Caroline stood before him in her candid corset, laced petticoat and a golden cascade of curls upon her bare shoulders.

Never had the sea been as tumultuous as their passion, a medley of lust and wantonness, of terror and guilt; the forbidden kindled them and desire melted them. The senses, repressed far too long, were unleashed at once like Aeolus's winds and inevitably, brought forth catastrophe.

The captain, totally mesmerised, didn't realise the impetus of the tempest nor heard the sailors' shouts. The ship was smashing against an insidious cliff as if steered by a diabolic hand.

Shortly afterwards, the merciless foamy vortex infested crew and lovers alike and the bodies, still with a grimace of terror on their faces, turned cold and swollen, forever doomed to their murky burial.

Inexplicably, part of the hull remained intact and still emerged from the water, the blackened prow glaring at the damned cliff. The main mast, although slightly reclined, stood guarding the relict, a lugubrious pole shrouded by the remains of the sails that seemed to attract the spectres of the drowned; their moans and cries could be heard in the surrounding hills and valleys, in the villages' huts and graveyards and woke up the living and the dead.

The story about the lovers in the captain's cabin, their ghosts embraced one to the other, spread quickly as though the angry mariners' phantoms had whispered the deadly secret into the ears of the bereft. It also reached Earl Joseph who was struck more by the insult than by the death of his fiancée, his vanity offended more than his honour. What grieved him most, though, was the loss of the countess's rich dowry.

As a matter of fact, the rumours of his depraved conduct were true and all his fortune had been dissipated in gambling, criminal affairs and precious gifts to his mistresses, the lascivious companions of his wild nights.

Since Joseph had turned as evil as the devil himself, he feared nothing and was determined to take revenge even if it should have led him to hell. The thought of fighting the supernatural diverted him and increased his arrogant conceitedness.

Furious, he set forth towards the village, but when he entered the local inn and searched for someone who would ferry him to the relict, everybody stepped away with awe, despite the copious retribution he offered.

A shady guy only fixed his bloodshot eyes on his and sneered, "I want more, buddy."

"No problem, I'll give you whatever you wish," he replied.

"I'm sure you will," the fellow sniggered, clapped him on the shoulder and led him to a nearby cove where a rickety boat was docked.

"I'll be there waiting for you no matter the time, man," he assured while untangling the ropes.

The part of the ship where the cabin was located wasn't totally submerged and Joseph took out his pistol ready to fire at the sinful spirits. No sooner he had reached it than languid laments resounded around him; the thought that they were still consuming their lustful encounter made him livid and he pushed open the door. On the berth were the poor limbs still clinging one to the other.

Blinded with fury, he was about to fire when Frederick's ghost leapt up and. exuding fetid drops from the lacerated bones, put his clammy hands around his throat, "How dares such a villain to come and disturb our peaceful sleep?"

Bold and fierce, the earl shouted, "How dare bloody cheaters talk about peace?"

"Better dead than your bride," cried Caroline. whose skeleton had risen and stepped by her lover's side.

"Heard what the lady just said?" sneered the captain and tightened the grip around the man's neck.

Immediately, an abnormal wave invaded the cabin and the nobleman was washed out of the vessel.

The bleak guy and his boat were there and as soon as the body appeared on the surface, he collected what he was after and sailed away.

When Joseph's corpse was found stranded on the shore, the marks of the choking were evident, but reasonable explanations hard to find.

However, they confirmed that the ship was haunted and fortified the belief that nobody should approach it if they cared for their lives and souls.

The God Of Blood And Bone

Michelle Ann King

The phone rings at three o'clock in the morning. It's on the coffee table, face down. Light leaks from underneath it. If I turn it over, it'll be flashing Vince's photo. At three o'clock in the morning, it's always Vince.

At least it didn't wake me up; one of the upsides of insomnia. There aren't many, so I've learned to take what I can get.

I look at the phone and the familiar fear crawls out of my chest: *does he know?*

We're good friends, that fear and I. It gnaws on my ribs, sticks icy claws into my heart. It'll freeze it before too long, kill it completely. But maybe that would be a kindness. No heart, no capacity to love. My family aren't built for love. It goes bad.

The phone is still buzzing. *Does he know?*

She wouldn't have told him, I'm sure of that. We agreed. And we're careful, so careful. But in this Age of Surveillance, who can be sure if it's enough? Secrets always get out, like mould seeping through damp plaster. I know this. God help me, I know this.

I put the phone to my ear and Vince says, 'Fuck's sake, Nick, where have you been?' He sounds angry, but no more than usual. Anger is my brother's default state.

211

I think about telling him I was asleep, but he probably wouldn't believe me and he definitely wouldn't care. Instead I just ask him what he wants.

'I want you to get over here and drive me to Islington. There's someone I need to go and see.'

'Now?'

'Yes, now. Why? You got something better to do?'

I could say yes. I could say I'm not doing this anymore. I could say I'm leaving, going to South America, to Australia, to Iceland. I check the price of flights twice a day. Two seats, one way.

'Nick? Did you hear me? I said, I've got somewhere to be.' His voice is rough and at least one bottle's worth of blurry.

I could say no. I could say I'm tired of being his chauffeur, his dogsbody. That I have a life, love and future of my own. On my own.

I could do that. I could.

'I'll be there in twenty minutes,' I say.

***

I'm actually the eldest by five minutes, although Vince tells it the other way. But five minutes doesn't give you much time to establish yourself, does it? And he's clearly the original, the vibrant, full-colour version. I'm the copy, grey-scale and faded. Our mother took us to a tarot reader when we were kids and she said that I had the older soul, a history of past lives that Vince never shared. Maybe that's what makes the difference; I'm diluted, Vince is fresh. Or maybe the old woman was just a scam artist. That probably makes just as much sense. I've tried using tarot cards, but they never told me anything I didn't know.

***

He's outside waiting when I arrive, bundled up in a parka and stamping his feet. I pull up and he gets in the passenger side, filling the car with the smell of smoke, whisky and rage. He gives me a piece of paper, creased and dirty, with an address written on it in handwriting I don't recognise. 'This is where we're going,' he says.

During the day the journey across London would take forever, but at this time of night the roads are swift and empty. Vince has five cars and never gets behind the wheel of any of them, but I've always enjoyed driving. There's a security, even if it's false, in the metal skeleton and the interplay of limbs and machinery. Car and driver give each other purpose.

Vince is quiet, his head resting on the side window as we swish through the dark. I've practically forgotten he's there when he says, 'Gemma's leaving me.'

My hand jerks on the wheel and we swerve slightly. 'What have you done?' I say. The words come out without thinking.

He stares at me. A muscle in his cheek jumps. 'Well, that's nice. So obviously, it has to be my fault? Thanks, Nick. Thanks for your sympathy. But for your information, I haven't done anything. Not a fucking thing.'

He probably even believes it. For Vince there are so many things, so many people, that simply don't count.

'I don't get it,' he says. 'Haven't I done everything for that woman? That fucking Merc cost forty grand. But it's not enough now?' His lips draw back from his teeth. He has them whitened and in the dim light it seems like they glow.

He pulls a pack of cigarettes out of his pocket and lights one. Turns it around in his fingers and watches it burn. 'She's not happy, apparently. Did you know that?'

I get as far as 'Vince—' and stop, because the air has solidified in my lungs. He doesn't seem to notice that I haven't actually answered and continues, 'Happy. What the hell is that supposed to mean, anyway? I've given her everything she ever asked for. And now I'm going to get all of it thrown back in my face.'

The cigarette drips ash onto the floor mat. I say, 'Vince,' again, but although my voice works this time I realise I have no idea what I'm going to say. It wasn't supposed to happen like this.

'You talk to her, don't you? What's she said? And for Christ's sake, watch where you're going.'

I correct the car's drifting course and ease off the accelerator. 'Nothing. She hasn't said anything. Not to me.'

He gives me a sharp look. 'You sure? Because she says there's no other bloke, but I don't believe that for a second. There's always another bloke. This hasn't come out of nowhere.'

'Yes. I'm sure.'

He leans back in the seat. 'Well, I'll find out. And when I do, he'll be sorry he ever strayed over this particular fence. And if he thinks he's going to be getting his hands on any of my money, he's going to be sorely disappointed. She's not walking out on me, making me look like a fucking prick and taking what I've earned with her. That is not going to happen. She's not going to get a single penny of my money. You understand me?'

I nod.

'Good. Because if I thought you knew something, if I thought you were covering something up, I'd be upset. You know that, don't you, Nick? You know that if you were to stand by and let that kind of shit go on, it wouldn't end well.'

I nod again. He looks at my hands, which are white on the steering wheel. I make an effort to relax them. His eyes are narrow and there's an edge of suspicion in them, but he says nothing else. He's not entirely satisfied, but I don't think he can quite make himself believe that I would cross him. That I would dare.

Do I believe it myself? It's a good question.

What did you think was going to happen? a voice in my head wants to know. *When you started fucking your brother's wife, how did you see that working out?*

Another good question. I'm full of them.

We drive in silence for another fifteen minutes until he taps on the dashboard. 'Here, this is it. Pull in over there.'

We're in a mainly residential area, with a small parade of shops at the top of the street. Three of the five shops are boarded up and all are dark. I swing the car into one of the marked bays and kill the engine.

Vince scrubs his hands over his face. The skin looks grey and loose. Unhealthy. 'Go in, will you, Nick? The one on the end. I'm supposed to see some woman called Alis. See if she's there.'

I get out and take a big gulp of air. It's not exactly fresh but it's better than inside the car. My hands are shaking and I shove them into my pockets. The nausea of adrenaline comedown floods my mouth with slimy, metallic-tasting saliva. I feel like I've narrowly avoided a car crash. No. I feel like I'm still having one.

The window of the shop is fogged with dirt and dust. I can just about make out a display of huge, boxy televisions that look like they should be in a museum. Hand-lettered signs, too faded to read, hang on wires above them.

I shoot a look at the car. Vince is leaning back, his eyes closed. I fumble my phone out of my pocket and call Gemma. A bad move, no doubt, but have I made any other kind?

It barely has a chance to ring before she answers. 'Nick? Where are you? Are you all right? Is he with you?'

'I'm fine. He's in the car. We're in Islington somewhere, I don't know why.' I never do.

Her voice trembles. 'I'm sorry. I know we said we'd wait, but I can't do it anymore. I didn't tell him about us, I didn't tell him anything. But I can't carry on living with him and pretending everything's all right. I can't.'

'It's okay. Don't worry. We'll sort it out.'

'I don't want to have to wait any more, Nick. I want to be with you.'

'I know. I do, too. And we will. We just have to be careful. Not yet. Soon. I promise. But not yet.'

I wait for her to ask when, and what exactly it is that we're waiting for and what my plan is. So many good questions.

I listen to her breathe for a while. Then she says, 'Okay. I love you,' and hangs up.

***

Does Vince deserve this?

Do I deserve her?

Does anyone get what they deserve?

***

I knock on the shop door and a woman answers. She's tiny, with cropped hair that looks white, but her face is unlined and she could be anywhere from a teenager to a grandmother. She nods when I ask if she's Alis, so I go back over to the car and get Vince.

Inside, the shop looks just as old and disused as it does outside. The main retail area is empty, with a single workbench pushed against the far wall, covered with a dust sheet. Alis leads us to a room at the back, this one kitted out like an office with a desk and three chairs in moulded orange plastic. A scratched metal filing cabinet leans against one wall and a bare bulb dangles from the ceiling. There's no

217

other furniture and no computer on the desk. The room feels both dated and oddly timeless. It suits her.

Vince pulls over one of the chairs and makes a show of brushing off the seat before he sits down.

'So you're an assassin,' he says. 'I've got to say, you're not exactly what I expected.'

Alis watches him with no expression. Her eyes are very pale and she blinks slowly and infrequently. 'That would be an advantage, no?'

I stare from her to my brother. 'Excuse me. What?'

Both of them ignore me. 'How do we do this, then?' Vince says.

'Half of the price is paid when the deal is agreed, the rest upon completion of the work.'

Vince pulls out his wallet and takes out four fifties. He holds them out. 'Five hundred quid. Seems cheap.'

She gives him a small smile. 'There are other compensations than money, Mr Rand, when you enjoy your work.'

He grins. 'Well, good for you.'

'Vince,' I say. 'What are you doing? What is this?'

Alis makes no move to take the money, so he throws it on her desk. Then he takes a photograph out of the wallet and drops it on top. Gemma, her hair pulled back in a ponytail and her hand up to shade her eyes against the sun. She's smiling.

'How do you do it?' Vince says. 'Do you shoot her, run her over, what? Do you do the job yourself, or sub-contract?'

Alis glances down at the photo. 'The method is immaterial. The work will be done.'

'You have to make sure it can't come back to me,' he says. 'I'll be the first one they look at. The husband always is. Especially if they find out she was going to leave me.'

'No suspicion will attach to you. That is guaranteed.'

'Then we've got a deal.'

She inclines her head. 'Agreed.'

I grab his arm. 'Vince. What are you doing?'

'Like I said, I'm going to be the first one they look at. So I can't use any of our own people, can I? It'd be asking for trouble. But don't panic, Alis here came highly recommended.' He shakes my hand off without looking at me. 'So there's nothing to worry about, is there, love?'

Alis smiles. She has fine features but full, wide lips that make her mouth seem too large for her face.

'I serve the God of Blood and Bone,' she says. 'I pray to my God and I am never disappointed. Others must take it on faith that their prayers are heard, but I have no need of faith. I have death.'

'If you say so,' Vince says. 'Well, we'll leave you to it, then. Pleasure doing business and all that. Come on, Nick.' He gets up and walks out without a backwards glance.

Alis is still sitting behind the desk, hands in her lap. The bare bulb above us flickers. The money and the photograph of Gemma are lying where Vince dropped them. 'Listen,' I say and reach out for the

219

photo, 'he's not thinking straight. He doesn't really—'

The photo curls up at the edges and smoke drifts upwards. A second later, a spike of white flame shoots up, blazing so brightly I have to close my eyes. Then it flashes out and disappears, leaving an after-image that dances behind my eyelids but no soot, residue or other marks on the metal surface of the desk. The photo and the money are gone.

'The deal has been made,' she says. 'The work will be done.'

I step backwards. My feet tangle in the legs of the chair and I go down hard. My teeth click together and I taste blood.

Under the desk, a huge rat pauses to stare at me before scurrying into the shadows at the edge of the room. More shadows than there were before, I'm sure.

I get to my knees and have to wait for the room to stop spinning before I can make it the rest of the way. When I manage to stand up straight, Alis is gone.

***

The sun comes up as we turn off the North Circular, but the sky is so stuffed with cloud it hardly makes any difference. When we get back to the house, we find all the lights are on.

Vince doesn't invite me in but I follow him anyway. Gemma is in the kitchen, fully dressed. She looks pale, but determined. A pot of coffee is brewing and a plate of toast lays untouched on the

220

table. The news is playing on the TV, with the sound down. Not that it matters. The story never changes.

Vince ignores her and stomps upstairs. She gives me a wide-eyed look and gets up. I shake my head and she lets him go.

'What happened?' she says, her voice low.

I shake my head again. 'Gem, this isn't the right time. Tell him you didn't mean it, you've changed your mind. Tell him you'll stay.'

Her jaw flexes as she clenches her teeth. 'No.'

'Gemma—'

'No. I can't. I know this is a mess and I'm not trying to push you. I'll wait for you, Nick. I said I would and I will. But not here. Not with him.'

I look past her shoulder, out the window. The trees are all barren and stripped. A mess. Yes.

'I know what you're thinking,' she says, 'but you haven't done anything wrong. This isn't a mistake.' She reaches out and runs her thumb over my cheekbone. 'But that's why I love you—that you can think it. Vince wouldn't be capable.'

I lean into her touch, but when I close my eyes all I can see is her face in the photo, curling and blackening.

Upstairs, Vince yells my name. Gemma and I both flinch.

Am I different from my brother? Yes.

Am I better?

I want the answer to be the same. But I don't know. I don't know.

I pull away from Gemma and head for the stairs. Vince is in the bedroom and it looks like he got halfway through changing his clothes before giving up.

'Phone Bill,' he says. 'Tell him to put the meeting with Heyward back to tomorrow. I can't face listening to him whining, not today. I'm knackered. And while you're about it, tell him to get me some of that Scotch from the club. The proper stuff. That blended shit gives you a rotten hangover.' He scrubs his hand over his face and yawns.

'Vince. Don't do this.'

He looks at me blearily. 'Heyward'll manage for another day. Since when were you bothered about what happens to him, anyway?'

'I'm not talking about Heyward.'

'Oh. Right. Look, I told you. It's fine. I know that Alis seems like a bit of a weirdo but I've got it on good authority that she knows what she's doing.'

'Don't,' I say again. 'If Gemma wants to go, can't you just—let her?'

He frowns. 'Since when were you so squeamish, since when do you tell me what to do and since when was this any of your fucking business? Huh? Since when, Nick?'

'Vince—'

'There something you want to tell me?'

I look away. 'No. I just—'

'Just what?'

Asking good questions runs in the family. I don't give him an answer. I don't have one.

He shakes his head and something I can't identify—contempt? Disappointment?—flashes in his eyes.

Maybe this whole thing was just a test, to see what I'd do. Maybe none of it was real. Maybe Alis is a plant, an actor. Maybe we still have time.

I try to believe this. I try very, very hard.

Vince sniffs and pulls a face. 'Now what? She's fucking burned something, hasn't she? I tell you, I'm going to be better off without her. I'll buy myself a cook and a prozzie and bang, straight away I'm better off on all fronts. Nick, go down and sort it out, will you? I feel like shit and I can't be doing with any of this today.'

I'm halfway down the stairs when the fire alarm goes off. I run the rest of the way. The kitchen is swirling with greasy smoke and the first thing I see is the frying pan on the stove, flames dancing on the glistening surface of the oil. The second thing is Gemma, stretched out on the floor. Her eyes are open and one arm is caught at an awkward angle underneath her. If there's any blood, it isn't visible against the black tiles.

I kneel beside her and shake her shoulder, call her name. Her head lolls and she doesn't respond. I thrust my fingers into the hollow under her jaw, but no pulse beats against my skin.

I scream for Vince, and when I look up he's there, throwing a tea towel over the smouldering pan.

'Call an ambulance,' I say.

I wait on the floor with her, cradling her head, until the paramedics make me move. They perform rituals familiar from a dozen medical dramas with quiet, calm efficiency. They lift her gently, treat her with care. But I see one look at the other, and give a tiny shake of his head.

***

Vince gets Bill to drive us both to the funeral. Nobody offers me their sympathy or condolences. Why would they? I'm just the brother-in-law.

I think I see Alis at the back of the crowd, her white hair stark against the dark shapes of the trees and the cars, but when I try to find her again, she's gone.

***

The kitchen's been scrubbed out by a professional firm, but it still smells of smoke and death. Some stains can't be disinfected away.

Vince opens a bottle of Scotch—the good stuff, from the club—and pours two generous measures into squat, thick-bottomed glasses. He holds one out to me, but I ignore it. He shrugs and puts it back on the table.

'Congratulations,' I say. 'A good job, well done. You must be pleased.'

He lifts his glass and empties it in one go. 'What are you talking about?'

'Gemma's murder.'

He shakes his head and refills the glass to a higher level. 'Gemma wasn't murdered. She died of a brain haemorrhage, remember? Natural causes.'

'So it can't come back on you, right? Just like she promised. Alis. And the God of Blood and Bone. You paid for it, they delivered.'

He rolls his eyes. 'What part of natural causes don't you understand? She wasn't killed, she just died. Sometimes that happens. People just die.'

'Not Gemma.'

'Fuck's sake, Nick. Let it go. It's finished.'

'Not quite,' says a voice from the doorway. 'The work has been done, now the payment is due.'

Vince jumps, slopping amber liquid over the rim of his glass. 'Jesus, how did you get in here?'

Alis is dressed as she was before, in dark jeans and a black hooded sweatshirt. She looks at Vince impassively. 'The payment is due.'

'You at it as well? Listen, my darling wife up and died of her own accord, so I don't owe you anything. Actually, I should get a refund. How about that, eh? Give me my two hundred and fifty back, since you didn't earn it.'

'I prayed to my God and He answered. Now you will pay.'

The smell of rotten, greasy smoke is getting worse. 'Do it,' I say. 'Pay her, Vince.' The words sit thick and unpleasant in my mouth.

'Are you kidding? What's the matter with you—the pair of you? Am I the only one who understands what a fucking brain haemorrhage is?'

'It is the visitation of my God,' Alis says.

'Yeah, nice try,' Vince says. 'Now get out.'

He turns his attention back to the whisky bottle. Alis doesn't move. The last sliver of late afternoon sun sinks below the roofline and the room dims

225

immediately. Next door's dog, which has been barking constantly, falls silent. The TV playing softly in the lounge clicks off. The wall clock stops.

The only sound I can hear is my own breathing echoing in my ears. The rest of the world has been muffled, wrapped in soft fog. It's in my ears, my nostrils, my throat. I can't breathe.

'Pay her,' I say again. 'Just pay her, Vince.' But I don't know if he hears me.

Full dark seems to have fallen in less than two minutes. Panic claws at me and I want to get out of here but Alis is shaking her head and I understand that there's nowhere to go. It's gone, all of it, drifted away like a waking dream. There's nothing outside. There's just this house, this room where Gemma died and the God of Blood and Bone.

'The transaction is incomplete,' Alis says. 'The agreement is broken. The work will be undone.'

Vince laughs. It's an ugly, braying sound. Everything about my brother is ugly. How did I not see this before?

'Undone?' he says. 'What's that supposed to mean? You going to bring her back, are you? That'll be a good one, I'd like to see that.'

Someone moans. I think it might be me. 'Don't,' I say, but Vince ignores me. When has he ever done anything else?

'Your wish is my command,' Alis says and gives him a tight little smile. The air in the room feels overheated, the hairs inside my nostrils crisping. We're going to burn, all of us.

'Look, if you don't—' Vince starts, then breaks off. 'Now where the fuck's she gone?'

226

My ears are still ringing, but the pressure's lifted and normal sounds—the dog, the ticking of the clock, the distant whoosh of traffic—have resumed. 'Back to hell,' I say.

He snorts, as if I've said something funny.

***

Vince takes the bottle of Scotch into his office and shuts the door. I lay on the floor where my love died, and wait.

The work will be undone.

She can do it, I have no doubt about that. Alis and her God can do anything. They took her, they can bring her back.

There's a knock on the door and Vince shouts for me to answer it.

Maybe when I do, I'll find Gemma there, smiling. She'll hug me and tell me that she loves me, that everything is going to be okay. That there's been a terrible mistake, or perhaps a miraculous recovery, but now it's over and we can forget about it and get on with our lives. And Vince will be so relieved that he'll forgive us both and give us his blessing. And we'll all live happily ever after.

I get up and go to the door. There's a dark shape through the glass.

Vince shouts again for me to answer it. I close my eyes, offer a prayer to the God of Blood and Bone and do what I'm told.

La Patasola Kills in Tierradentro

Shashi Kadapa

It came out of the Tierradentro the underground funeral caves where the ancient Inca priests had held it with spells. It hopped on its one leg over the debris and through the trees to the mining camp that had disturbed its spell. After centuries it was hungry, thirsted for human flesh and blood, and it was coming to get them. It was the La Patasola.

It starts killing

Santiago sat on guard, bored and angry. Thoughts of young del putas, fufurufa, prostitutes in downtown bars in Bogotá city filled his mind. He jerked up when he heard a female singing in the night. He picked up a miner's helmet with a torch and went after the voice.

The voice receded and he followed. She was hiding behind a tree and in the torchlight, he saw a slender girl with white skin standing with her nude back partly turned towards him. He could see one bulging breast with the sharp nipple poking up. Mad with lust, he dropped his rifle, pulled her out and she fell into her arms.

Santiago felt the skin shrivel and sag and he smelled rotting corpses. Frightened, he let go and looked at the figure that had turned towards him.

The face was a grinning skull. She had only one breast, one eye bulged out, the nose hooked, the lips thick and a forked tongue flicked over sharp and long incisors.

Fear was paralyzing, she wrapped her arms around him and sank her fangs in his neck. His head bent down and, even through the intense pain, he could see only one leg that ended in a hoof. He could feel his blood being sucked out and his organs drying up.

The miners found him next morning. He looked like a dry banana skin, blood and organs drained out as he lay like a grotesque wrinkled and deflated balloon.

It rises

Kalku, the curandero from the village had warned. "This is the land of the Incas, cursed, many evil spirits roam the forests. Do not disturb the earth here. Vile demons are held with spells in underground caves. They will rise and come to eat you alive."

The gold mining and lumber camp set up near the village of San Andres de Pisimbala in Andes, Columbia, was busy. Rocks were blasted, crushed, leached with acid to bring up tiny slivers of elusive gold. Shock waves travelled a long distance through the rocks, disturbing and breaking things many miles away.

Gustavo, the lead miner, stepped out on a rock and looked, worried, at the vast vista before him. Smoke climbed from the volcano and legends said that the volcano would blow if evil befell the land.

Garcia, the refinery boss, shouted at the laborers, "Bury him. Work, else I will throw you into the jungle."

A rumble and mild earthquake shocks made the ground tremble. Smoke from the volcano grew stronger.

***

Gustavo approached the curandero sitting under a tree in the village and smoking a cocaine pipe.

"O elder Kalku, you are as old as the mountains. What killed Santiago?"

"La Patasola."

"What?"

"It is the evil spirit, more than a thousand years old, of a woman called Pachama. Her husband, a brave warrior called Apo Yupanqui, fed up with her infidelity, cut her leg and sealed her in the underground funeral cave, the Tierradentro. The blasting opened the cave and she now wanders in the night to kill. People call her the La Patasola."

"What can we do to stop it?"

"I will try to trap her and need an assistant. Will you help?"

Gustavo reluctantly nodded his head.

La Patsola kills again

She killed three more that night. Rodriguez was drunk and sitting in his cabin when he saw a woman

230

pass by his window. He got up hurriedly and she stood under a tree, lit by the perimeter lamp. Rodriguez rushed, stumbling and falling at her feet. He looked at the single leg and then claw-like hands lifted him, teeth sank in his back, draining his blood.

Lopez died when he went to relieve himself and Hernandez was drained as he worked. This was too much and the laborers deserted the camp in the morning.

***

Joaquín and his assistant Garcia drank heavily and worked themselves into an angry frenzy.

Joaquín lurched drunkenly, "She comes in the night? I will shoot and hang her corpse on a tree." Fully drunk, Garcia toppled over and started snoring. Gustavo sat in his cabin, peering out of the window, very frightened.

The singing came softly and Joaquín lunged forward, shining his torch in the darkness. There! He could make out the nude back hidden under creepers. He fired the buckshot, got her in the back. He shone his torch and could see her on the ground, gaping bullets in the back but there was no blood.

"Ah, bitch. I got you now."

He kicked it in the back and then screamed when his foot sank into flesh and suckers bit his leg and drained him. Gustavo saw with wide eyes as she hopped on one foot, settled on Garcia and drank him.

231

Then she leaped and was gone. He did not know why she had not come for him.

Entering the Tierradentro

Gustavo rushed to village to meet Kalku, who was sleeping in his hut. He stuttered and stammered and narrated the killings. Kalku comforted him and said. "We have to find the Tierradentro and seal the cave now. La Patasola has fed and will sleep."

"Where do we find the cave?"

"I know. Let us go."

"Why did she not kill me?"

"Maybe she thinks you are good."

***

A red glow appeared near the peak, acrid smoke filled the forest and the volcano would erupt soon. Villagers ran to their boats and paddled downstream to safety.

Gustavo picked up a few torches from the camp and a gun while Kalku lit a fire torch. He had a stick with bird feathers and a rope.

The cloying atmosphere with dripping weaving creepers and trees was very petrifying. He feared the shadows that clung to the trees and moved with the breeze. The flame from Kalku's torch danced in the shadows, creating psychedelic patterns. Shining eyes of small animals glared back.

An owl suddenly took off silently and Gustavo lifted his gun when the wings brushed his head. He feared the evil spirit more than anything and he imagined that every tree hid her.

***

The sulfur fumes were very strong and Gustavo gasped with difficulty. He could feel tremors and shocks as the volcano shuddered.

He whispered, "Should we not run away to safety? We can always come back."

Kalku shushed him and they continued. Páez River flowed from a lake in a plateau just above them. The area above the plateau was very steep with hard rocks and lava flows with straggly growth of shrubs.

Kalku said, "It has been more than eight hundred years since the volcano was active."

"What? How do you know?"

Kalku continued, "If the spirit is trapped inside the cave, the lava will cover her forever."

They continued up the mountain and walked to the lake. Kalku moved to the bank and shone his torch at a boat tied at the edge. "If Nevado del Huila starts erupting, jump into the boat and row away fast."

He motioned Gustavo to move forward and pointed at an opening in the rocks. A large stone that acted like a seal had cracked from the force of the dynamite blasting at the mine. Further tremors had shattered it. He could see strange marking on the rocks and skeletons of human scarifies on the ground. What was buried inside?

Kalku whispered, "La Patasola is buried here. Be careful and hide behind a pillar. When I shout, tie it with this sacred rope and I will use spells to bind it. This talisman will protect you."

"What, me? How do I tie it?"

Kalku handed a lasso and a talisman on a chain that Gustavo wore around his neck.

The volcano had becoming very active and the tremors were rumbling through the rocks. He could see the rim red with lava poised ready to pour. The cave was directly in the path.

They descended into the cave and crept down the winding steep steps that led to the burial chambers. A stale and foul smell of many centuries hit Gustavo and he choked. He switched on his torch and looked at the strange colored patterns on the walls. Murals of Supay, Saqra and other gods in their bestial finery and long teeth gazed at him with arms raised to grab him. The atmosphere was claustrophobic and he felt the walls closing in.

They trap the La Patasola

Kalku stopped inside the last chamber and shone his torch inside. Gustavo saw something on the platform, pale skin shone in the light. It was the La Patasola.

It was turning and he could see the cut leg, one breast and then it sat upright on the platform. She was grinning through her ghastly and misshapen face, the tongue flicked out, one eye gone and the other popping out, the sharp teeth hung over the lips and she licked them.

Kalku motioned to Gustavo to hide behind the doorway and stood staring at the creature.

He said, "Ah Pachama. You vile woman, you have risen again."

Gustavo was stunned when she replied, "Yes, Apo Yupanqui, my husband. Your spell broke when the cover stone broke. This time you will be trapped here and I will hunt forever."

Gustavo gasped in wonder. This Kalku was the warrior and husband of this evil? After so many centuries it was alive?

She started singing in her soft voice and advanced on Kalku who slowly stepped back drawing her out. When she was out of the chamber entrance, he shouted, "Throw the rope. Tie her!"

She screamed in anger at the betrayal and tuned towards Gustavo with her mouth open but the talisman protected him. He threw the lasso over her head and arms, tightening the rope. She threshed with anger and would have broken free but Kalku brought out his wand and threw holy ash on her, then started uttering old Inca chants.

She became quiet and fell down. The volcano burst just then and the walls started crumbling, the roof was crumbling.

Kalku shouted to Gustavo, "Run! Save yourself."

The break in the chant revived her and she reach out to grasp Kalku with her arms, her thigh was wrapped around his torso and he lay on her, clasping her tight like a lover in a sexual embrace.

Gustavo ran out, scrambling over the steps and stumbling into the open.

Gustavo escapes

Gustavo looked as the volcano erupted and through the acrid smoke he could see lava flowing down the slopes. He had seconds to escape and he ran, sliding over the rocks, scraping his back and arms. His clothes were smoldering and the intense heat scalded his eyes and lungs. The lake was just ahead and the boat rocked with the tremors.

He jumped into the boat, untied the rope, pulled at the oars and peered at the cave. It was smothered with hot lava, sealing the two of them forever.

Lava hit the waters on the other end, sending a huge wave and his boat was carried on. It glided into the rapid waters of the foaming river and went over the rocks. His head hit the side and he passed out.

He woke to the chatter of natives downstream who helped him out. There was no trace of volcano or the spirit. Who would believe him?

He felt something poking his neck and saw the talisman. So it was true and he had helped to trap the La Patasola.

How long would it remain trapped?

Meet the authors:

Dan Allen is Canadian and enjoys spending time in Northern Ontario. You can find his short stories in numerous magazines, anthologies, and podcasts. Visit www.danallenhorror.com to see a presentation of his published work.

His terrifying look at Alzheimer's, "Above the Ceiling," is featured in Bards and Sages collection of the Best Indie Speculative Fiction Vol. 2.

A personal favourite, "Sympathy for the Zingara," can be found in the March 2019 edition of ParAbnormal Magazine.

His terrifying story, "The Basement" (edited by Horror Zine's Jeani Rector), was published by Hellbound Books in July 2020.

You can visit Dan at www.danallenhorror.com and follow him on Facebook and Twitter at

@danallenhorror. You can write to Dan at contact@danallenhorror.com

Olivia Arieti lives in Torre del Lago Puccini, Italy, with her family. She writes drama, poetry and fiction. Her stories have appeared in several magazines and anthologies including, *Enchanted Conversations, Enchanted Tales Literary Magazine, Fantasia Divinity Magazine, Forgotten Tomb Press, Horrified Press, Infective Ink, Pandemonium Press, Sirens Call Publications, Blood Song Books, Black*

Hare Press, Pussy Magic Magazine, Stormy Island Publishing, Breaking Rules Publishing, Scarlet Leaf Review, Iron Faerie Publishing, Dark Dossier Magazine, Paramour Ink Press, Raven and Drake Publishing.

Justin Boote is an Englishman living in Barcelona and has been writing for five years. In this time, he has published around forty short stories in diverse magazines and anthologies, including ten for Scare Street's Night Terror series, a novelette called Badass with Terror Tract Publishing, two short story collections on Amazon called Love Wanes, Fear is Forever, Volumes 1 and 2, and numerous short stories.

He has also written a trilogy to be published in the summer and is currently finishing a five-book series, while also outlining another.

He can be found at his Facebook author page https://www.facebook.com/BooteJustin

Gary Budgen lives and works in London. His previous work has appeared in various magazines including Interzone, BFS Horizons, Morpheus Tales, Sein und Werden and the BFS Award short-listed anthology Humanagerie from Eibonvale. His work has been in many other anthologies from publishers including Thirteen O'Clock Press, Boo Books and Horrified Press. A collection of stories, Chrysalis, is published by Horrified Press and the chapbook Fragments of Onyx by Salo Press. A full publishing history can be found at garybudgen.wordpress.com.

Dorothy Davies is an editor, writer, photographer and medium. Somehow all these things come together in her seemingly crowded leisure and work life. She is an avid kindle user, and delights in writing reviews for Amazon, especially when a novel is deleted a mere 2-3 chapters in and is too badly written to be read… she retired from editing for a while to run a second hand shop, the best one on the Isle of Wight, but the thrill of finding and publishing outstanding stories became too much so she started again with the Gravestone Press imprint. She still runs the shop…

Joseph Dowling has pursued many interests and diverse career paths, always knowing he would write seriously one day.

In 2020, now owner of a small but previously thriving chain of retro arcade bars temporarily shuttered due to Covid-19, he fell into an obsession.

Since finding the passion, Joseph can't imagine life without the stories constantly rattling around his head. Eager to make up for lost time, he's in the habit of writing every day, becoming a keen student of the craft. He recently had his first acceptance and will appear in an upcoming anthology called 'Worlds Collide'.

Jim Dyar grew up in the deeper part of Maine and says he has always been a bit disturbed. He has been a professional ghost hunter, a comic book artist and is the author of the From the Minds of Humanity books, an Action / Humor series that caused several people to encourage him to write Horror. Most days he can be found researching the Paranormal, chatting with the voices in his head, or simply enjoying rowing on the swelling tide of human misery.

Paul Edwards is a life-long horror fan and writes his own twisted tales in any spare time that he can grab. He has seen three collections of stories published – *Now That I've Lost You* (Screaming Dreams), *Black Mirrors* (Rainfall Books) and *Night Voices* (Demain Publishing), the latter being a joint-collection with author Frank Duffy. Paul is also a fan of role-playing games, rock music and rough Somerset cider.

R.G. Evans is the author of the poetry books *Overtipping the Ferryman, The Holy Both,* and *Imagine Sisyphus Happy,* as well as the horror novella *The Noise of Wings.* His poems, fiction and nonfiction, have appeared in *SurVision* (Ireland), *Rattle,* and *Weird Tales* among other publications. His collection of original songs, *Sweet Old LIfe*, is available on most streaming platforms. Recently retired after thirty-four years of high school teaching, Evans teaches creative writing at Rowan University in New Jersey, USA. Website: www.rgevanswriter.com

Joseph Genius writes horror, less to entertain and more to scar. He writes not only for income, he writes because he is a writer. Joseph is Cebuano-American and he has lived in, worked in, and traveled extensively throughout both nations, a unique experience behind a unique voice. Connect with Joseph: info@josephgenius.com

Michael H. Hanson created the ongoing SHA'DAA shared-world anthology series currently consisting of "SHA'DAA: TALES OF THE APOCALYPSE", "SHA'DAA: LAST CALL","SHA'DAA: PAWNS," "SHA'DAA: FACETS", "SHA'DAA: INKED", "SHA'DAA: TOYS," and "SHA'DAA: ZOMBIE PARK", all published by Moondream Press (an imprint of Copper Dog Publishing). Michael's short story "C.H.A.D." appears in the Crystal Lake Publishing anthology "C.H.U.D. LIVES!", his short story "Rock and Road" appears in the Roger Zelazny tribute anthology "SHADOWS AND REFLECTIONS," and his short story "Born Of Dark Waters" appears in the Independent Legions Publishing anthology "THE BEAUTY OF DEATH 2: DEATH BY WATER." Michael also has stories in Janet Morris's Heroes in Hell (HIH) anthology volumes, "LAWYERS IN HELL," "ROGUES IN HELL," "DREAMERS IN HELL," "POETS IN HELL," "DOCTORS IN HELL," "PIRATES IN HELL," "LOVERS IN HELL," and "MYSTICS IN HELL." He has had over 100 short stories published in the fields of science fiction, fantasy and horror and he has written and published six collections of poetry, "AUTUMN BLUSH" and "JUBILANT WHISPERS" (Racket River Publishing),"DARK PARCHMENTS" and "WHEN THE NIGHT OWL SCREAMS" (MoonDream Press), and "ANDROID

241

GIRL And Other Sentient Publications" and "QUARANTINE WORLD: Trapped in The Coronaverse" (Three Ravens Publishing).

Kevin Jones has written many stories for the horror world, and contributes a scary little story about a demon for Blood Clots.

Thomas Leaf lives in a house with an unpleasant basement, he has no pets, he practices his smile almost every day and has been scrawling words in various notebooks - both lined, and unlined - for some years now.

Some of his writing makes sense.

As a founding member of the Alcalet Archive, Thomas knows that he should be engaging with people on social media whilst developing an effortlessly intriguing bio.

He can't right now - he's too busy writing the kind of stories he would like to read.'

Terrance V. Mc Arthur is a storyteller, puppeteer, magician, balloon artist, basketmaker, and a retired librarian. His stories have been anthologized by Thirteen O'clock Press, Untreed Reads, and Trembling With Fear.

Rickey Rivers Jnr was born and raised in Alabama. He is a Best of the Net nominated writer and cancer survivor. His work has appeared in the JJ Outre Review, Stellium Literary Magazine, Fabula Argentea (among other publications).

Rie Sheridan Rose multitasks. A lot. Her short stories appear in numerous anthologies, including Killing It Softly Vol. 1 & 2, Hides the Dark Tower, Dark Divinations, and On Fire. She has authored twelve novels, six poetry chapbooks, and lyrics for dozens of songs. She is also editor-in-chief for Mocha Memoirs Press and editor for the Thirteen O' Clock imprint of Horrified Press. She tweets as @RieSheridanRose.

Chris Rodriguez has retired from the horrors of conventional life. She now lives on the brink of inspiration in a 100-year-old cottage in Pocatello, Idaho. Her works have appeared in various themed anthologies including Rhetoric Askew, several by Horrified Press/Thirteen O'Clock, Left Hand Publisher's, *Mindscapes Unimagined*, ParABnormal Magazine, DL Russell's *Nobody Goes Out Anymore* and Blunder Woman Productions, *Wrong Turn,* which has recently won Best Audiobook Anthology at the SOVAS Awards. You can find her latest at https://www.chrisrodriguez-onthebrink.com or https://www.amazon.com/author /chrisrodriguez-onthebrink.

E. S. Sibbald is a young writer working in the library and education industry. They remain alive only by devouring words and worlds. When not living in their own mind, they reside in Sydney, Australia. They can be found on twitter at @essibbald.

Edmund Stone is a writer, poet and artist who spins tales of strange worlds and horrifying encounters with the unknown. He lives in a quaint town on the Ohio River with his wife, a son, four dogs and two mischievous cats. You can contact him at edmundstoneauthor.com,

SJ Townend hopes that her stories take the reader on a journey to often a dark place and only sometimes back again.

SJ won the Secret Attic short story contest (Spring 2020), has had fiction published with Sledgehammer Lit Mag, Hash Journal, Ghost Orchid Press, Bandit Fiction, Black Hare Press, Black Petals Horror Magazine, Ellipsis Zine, Gravely Unusual, Gravestone Press, Holy Flea, Horla Horror, and was long listed for the Women on Writing non-fiction contest in 2020.

She has also written and self-published two dark mystery novels, both of which are available to purchase on Amazon: (Tabitha Fox Never Knocks, Twenty-Seven and the Unkindness of Crows).

Follow her on Twitter: @SJTownend

Michelle Ann King is a short story writer from Essex, England. Her stories of fantasy, science fiction, crime, and horror have appeared in over a hundred different venues, including Strange Horizons, Interzone, Black Static, and Orson Scott Card's Intergalactic Medicine Show. Her collections are available in ebook and paperback from Amazon and other online retailers, and links to

her published stories can be found at her website:
www.transientcactus.co.uk